The Mobster's Mate

Kiki Clark

 Created with Vellum

A human mob boss and an injured jaguar shifter brought together by a cruel enemy... and fate.

Caden hasn't believed in fated mates since he was a cub. He figures it's more of a fairytale that shifter parents tell their kids than the reality of what passes for mates in some of the packs he's seen.

But then he comes face-to-face with a human man who smells like orange blossoms and radiates authority and safety.

And Caden... Well, he hasn't felt safe in a long time.

While the rest of the world fears and reviles Quinten Amato and the things he does under the guise of his business, Caden is drawn to him like a cub to an alpha. He doesn't care what anyone says or what Quinten does, he and his jaguar know the kind of man he is.

The kind who saved his life.

The kind who comforts him when he wakes up terrified.

The kind whose calm commands set his blood on fire.

Convincing his bossy human they're meant to be together isn't going to be easy. Especially not when Quinten's certain Caden needs things he can't get from him—and that being a part of Quinten's life in the shadows is too dangerous.

And he might be right.

The Mobster's Mate is a full-length novel featuring a human with questionable morals and a jaguar shifter who only sees the best in him. You'll find an age gap, found family vibes, fated mates, and gobs of possessiveness.

This title is a standalone novel set within the Kincaid Pack universe. It can be read and enjoyed on its own. However, if you'd like to understand the nuances of the world, then start your journey with The Alpha and His King (Kincaid Pack Book 1).

For all my readers who wished that Rick had done more than just taken a couple of hands...
This one is for you.

Author's Note

Writing Quinten and Caden's story was an interesting challenge. Because the story is set within the Kincaid Pack Universe, there are some obvious expectations from readers who have loved those books—but I also wanted new readers to be able to step in and enjoy it without having to commit to reading a six-book prequel.

I hope I've accomplished that and given everyone a story they can fully enjoy. These two are so special to me and I'm very excited for you to read their journey to their HEA.

Below is a content warning for the book and contains information I would definitely consider a spoiler. If you are sensitive to blood or discussions of past physical abuse, please read and take any precautions you need to protect yourself.

-Kiki

CONTENT WARNING:

This book contains a semi-descriptive conversation between the two main characters about the physical and medical torture one endured while being held captive over several months before the book takes place.

(This character does not seek the help of a mental health professional—please remember this is fiction and not meant to be a guide in healing from trauma.)

There are also multiple on-page deaths (all baddies) and mentions of blood, including blood drinking by a vampire.

Please be kind to yourself and proceed with caution if any of these topics are triggering for you.

If you have questions, please don't hesitate to email me at kiki@kikiclark.com.

Chapter One

"**D**on't get pissed at me. This is a fucking courtesy call because you helped me save Kincaid's life."

Quinten Amato ground his teeth to keep from snapping at the infuriating man. Gabriel Morde's deep Southern drawl was giving him the urge to smash his fist through the wall or take a crowbar to the phone sitting on his office desk, but Morde wasn't *wrong*. And that made everything worse.

Regardless, no one spoke to him like that and lived. Too bad the Kincaid Pack seemed to do whatever the fuck they wanted, consequences be damned.

Quinten was really beginning to wonder if having a man as powerful as Kincaid owe him a favor was worth keeping him from dying. If he hadn't sent his helicopter and the alpha had died, his life would be a hell of a lot less complicated these days.

When he didn't respond, he heard a deep sigh, and then Gabriel said, "Listen, Q, the world is changing—"

"Because you and your damn pack *changed* it," he snarled, blood heating. Gabriel's alpha, Rick Kincaid, had started a war with the shifter Council, the governing body of all parahumans in North America. Which would have been none of Quinten's business or concern, except Kincaid had basically nuked the Council off the map and was rebuilding from scratch a new, *democratic* government and sending the parahuman world into a damn tailspin. "You didn't like how things were, so you decided to fuck over the rest of us."

Gabriel scoffed. "Do you seriously expect me to apologize for what we did? The Council was corrupt as hell, and you and I know that better than most. I'm not sorry for making the world safer for parahumans, even if it's bad for your business."

He sneered at his desk phone and leaned back in his well-padded executive chair located in his enormous corner office on the top floor of the high-rise housing his multimillion-dollar business, Amato Imports. The company was a well-oiled machine run by some of the brightest execs money could buy so Quinten could keep the majority of his focus on... his other pursuits.

And that's where he kept butting up against Gabriel's pack.

The dissolution—or demolition, depending on who you asked—of the Council had been amazing for Quinten's less-than-ethical transactions. Kincaid's new, self-righteous group of do-gooders getting all up in his business was what was pissing him the fuck off. Running his tongue against his teeth, he said, "Damn, Morde. You've gotten soft now that you're getting your dick wet in a couple—"

"Watch it."

Finding the soft spot to press with shifters—or those mated to them in Gabriel's case since the man was as human as Quinten—was incredibly easy. But riling up Gabriel wasn't the point of the phone call, so he didn't continue, deciding against bringing the hunter's mates into the conversation again.

"I'm not giving up any aspect of *any* of my businesses because you and your alpha are suddenly squeamish." Not after everything he'd sacrificed while building his empire. Rick Kincaid and his lackeys would have to tear it out of his hands and then kill him because that would be the only way he'd give up the power he'd spent a decade and a half accumulating.

"The Guardians won't look the other way like the Council did."

Quinten rolled his eyes and pushed to his feet, buttoning his suit jacket. He had better things to do than listen to idle threats. "Your *Guardians* will take years to get up and running with any sort of real efficiency or authority. It's already been over ten months, and it's still pure chaos in the parahuman world. You may think you've done everyone a favor by dismantling the old system, but that doesn't change the fact that a lot of packs and covens still require the products and services *I* provide."

"They need protection and stability, not a glorified mobster."

The words hung in the air as he closed his hands into fists. If Gabriel had been standing in front of him, he doubted he would have been able to stop himself from laying the man out. Considering Gabe used to *kill people for money*, he had some fucking nerve.

Then again, Gabe had always been good at finding weak spots too.

He leaned forward and planted his knuckles on his mahogany desk, hovering over his phone. "Fuck you."

"Quinten—"

"Next time someone in your pack is dying, don't even think about coming to me for help."

"Q, come on—"

He picked up the phone receiver and then slammed it back down.

Glorified mobster.

Jaw tight, he stormed out of his office. The sigils etched around the doorway glowed as he passed through before fading back to nothing, hidden from sight unless you knew what to look for. His witches had insisted on them after the last death threat he'd received, and he'd caved when Ginger —their ringleader and pain in his ass—had said she'd call his brother and tell Liam about the threats if he didn't let her make some changes to his security.

Damn witch didn't fight fair. She knew he'd do just about anything to protect his baby brother, even from worrying about Quinten.

The sigils wouldn't stop a particularly powerful shifter or witch from coming through, but they'd notify Ginger and the others of the danger. He wasn't sure what use that would be since he'd probably still be dead if they were strong enough to break through the warding, but it made her feel better and got her off his back.

He'd always known the risks of his life and was under no illusions he'd die of old age. The fact that he was pushing forty and still alive, even though he tangled with unruly shifters every day?

Goddamn miracle.

He slammed his office door shut behind him, and his new assistant looked up from her computer, took one look at his face, and ducked her head down behind her computer, nothing showing but the top of her high ponytail. He curled his lip at her as he stormed past without a word, heading for his private elevator. She wasn't going to last any longer than the last three assistants HR had sent him.

Not for the first time, he wished Marge hadn't retired.

She'd been his dad's assistant before Quinten took over Amato Imports and stayed with him for years, providing a steadying hand as he'd taken the business his dad had left him and expanded it. And then expanded again into... less conventional areas.

And less legal.

Definitely less ethical.

Mafia... *adjacent.*

Marge may not have known all the things he was doing, but she never questioned him, never feared him, and never needed extra directions. Hell, half the time, she'd known what he needed before he had. If he hadn't known for certain otherwise, he would have sworn she was a seer.

And now, he was stuck with these young, terrified assistants who could barely last longer than a fiscal quarter.

Stepping into the elevator, he didn't react as a large man joined him, seeming to appear out of nowhere. As soon as the mirrored doors shut, Darius raised his scarred brow at him in the reflection, letting him know the wolf had overheard his phone call with Morde.

"We may need to make arrangements if Kincaid and his people are going to keep sticking their noses in our business," Quinten said, keeping his eyes forward and watching the numbers fall as they descended.

Darius's mouth twitched, and Quinten sighed.

"Just say it."

"He has a lot of support. Could get messy." Darius's voice was low and raspy, stating what they both knew. Kincaid wasn't just some chirpy asshole who didn't know how to mind his own business. He had the strongest pack on the continent and a lot of allies.

Quinten had no interest in going to war with him.

"I wasn't suggesting we send Nero to kill him," Quinten said dryly.

Darius grunted and straightened his shoulders as they neared their destination, the building's underground garage. He stepped halfway in front of Quinten as the doors slid open. "Make things easier."

Quinten smiled for the first time since Gabriel's name had popped up on his phone. Darius's bloodthirsty nature had that effect on him. "Maybe. It would definitely solidify me as the devil in a lot of people's eyes."

"Win-win."

Quinten chuckled and followed him to where his driver already had the SUV running and waiting for them, Darius having let him know they were on their way down before Quinten even left his office. "We'll cross that bridge if we need to. Until then, we need to button things up and make sure we're secure on all fronts in case they decide to try and force my hand."

Darius opened the back door and stepped out of the way so Quinten could climb inside ahead of him. He paused though, meeting his friend's stormy eyes. He barely noticed the scar traversing his face anymore, from his hairline through his left eyebrow and down to the corner of his mouth, giving him a permanent sneer and clouding his left eye.

But even with only one good eye, Quinten would never trust anyone more at his back.

"Things are going to change, but we won't," Quinten said softly, reaching up to grip the side of Darius's neck. The fact that the giant wolf not only allowed the touch but leaned into it a little each time always blew him away. The trust went both ways, and that humbled him. "No matter what, our people will stay protected. This is our city, our family."

"Our pack," Darius added, earning an exasperated look.

Shifters. They always thought with a pack mentality.

"I'm no alpha," he said, not for the first time. He gave Darius's neck a squeeze and then got into the SUV. "But if Kincaid tries to come for us and what we've built, he'll be very, very sorry."

Darius slid in next to him, patting Alan on the shoulder as soon as the door was closed to let the driver know they were ready to head out. They fell into silence as they exited the garage and joined the millions of others headed home for the evening.

The sun was setting, but Chicago was alive and thrumming all around them, the residents fully thawed from the harsh winter and enjoying every minute of the mild spring weather. Quinten watched the people they passed, thinking about his phone call with Morde and how he'd come to be where and who he was.

Growing up, he'd been just like so many other humans, oblivious to the parahuman world surrounding them. His dad was a successful owner of an import/export business and his mom a cardiothoracic surgeon. He'd grown up with nannies and tutors, but they'd still doted on him, and he'd been secure in his place in the world.

Everything changed when he was eleven.

One day, they were a family, and the next...

His dad left him and his mom three weeks after meeting a woman named Callie. Quinten was so angry, and so was his mom. Neither of them understood what had happened, why they were broken and bleeding. Why his dad had chosen another woman and her son over them.

He would remember his dad sitting him down and explaining as best he could about how Callie was his other half. His *mate*. How she and her son were *different*.

Different. That's how his old man had tried to explain shifters to him.

All Quinten heard was that they were *better*. He and

7

his mom were ordinary and not worth sticking around for, not when his dad could have a new and improved family.

His mom had gotten over it within a few months, focusing on building her career and lavishing attention on him, and even became friends with his dad and Callie eventually. It had been hard for Quinten to swallow at first, the idea that she hadn't actually been as happy as he'd thought and had started to thrive once she was single. All these years later, she was still operating, occasionally dating, and generally just living her best life.

Quinten... had taken a little longer to get to a good place with his dad.

He was furious at the man for ruining their family. God, he'd been a dramatic little shit. He wouldn't visit his dad unless he would guarantee Callie and her son wouldn't be there. He'd started getting into fights at school. Typical kid bullshit.

Quinten smiled, unseeing the passing scenery out the SUV's window.

It was almost a whole year after his dad met Callie that Quinten met her four-year-old son, Liam. Fuck, he'd been a cute little kid, and he'd looked at Quinten like he'd hung the moon. Followed him around that whole weekend, asked him a million questions.

Stole his damn heart.

And taught him what it meant to be family. To be *pack*.

The fact that Quinten spent the majority of his life now surrounded by shifters and witches who answered to him was an irony that wasn't lost on him.

He laid a hand over his phone in his pocket. When was the last time he'd talked to Liam? Maybe he'd call him when he got home and guilt him into coming for a visit. He hadn't seen him in person in nearly a year, and that just wasn't acceptable.

8

Maybe he should tell Alan to bring him to the private airport where he kept his jet and just go visit his baby brother and his pack of felines.

His phone was halfway out of his pocket, mouth opening to give the order, when Darius raised his own cell to his ear and grunted a greeting. The low growl that filled the interior of the vehicle raised the hairs on the back of his neck, the primitive part of his brain warning him of the dangerous predator.

Sighing, he shoved his phone away and waited to hear what new problem he'd have to deal with instead of harassing his brother.

"Hang on," Darius said, then muted the call and met Quinten's eyes. "Someone broke into one of the warehouses."

Quinten raised his brows. He could only assume it was someone new to town or maybe an unhoused person looking for shelter. "Send one of—"

"Ginger and Dominic are there with a few others. Dom says we need to get down there."

Quinten felt Alan's attention on them, but the fox kept his mouth shut, waiting to see what Quinten decided. He resisted the urge to rub at the headache forming behind his eyes. If it was just him and Darius, he wouldn't care about showing such weakness, but he was more careful around everyone else who worked for him.

He gave a single nod to Darius before turning his head away once more, annoyed he had to personally go and see whatever was happening in one of his warehouses instead of going home and...

And what?

He ignored the snide voice in his head pointing out he had no one waiting for him in his fancy penthouse. No pet. No plants.

He squinted at his window. He might actually have a plant, but his housekeeper took care of it, not him.

The only thing waiting for him at home was his sinfully large shower and the latest season of his favorite baking competition show.

If all the people who thought he was evil personified could see the sad state of his personal life, they'd probably be a lot less afraid of him.

Though that would be a mistake.

"Did he say why exactly I'm dragging myself all the way across town to the warehouse district?" Quinten asked mildly after a few minutes.

"Not really," Darius growled, still all prickly. "Just said you needed to see something."

"Hm." Dominic wasn't exactly one to scare easily. He'd originally come from a large, violent pack—he'd fought to stay alive nearly every day of his life until he left and made his way to Chicago and into Quinten's employment.

But he would *not* be happy if this was about some poor vagrant hunkering down amidst their pallets and refusing to leave.

Traffic had thinned out considerably by the time they pulled up to the warehouse, and he easily spotted Dominic's tall frame next to Ginger's curvy one right by the entrance. It looked like they were arguing, and that set his nerves on edge a lot more than Darius's renewed growls. Like most mated pairs, the two were disgustingly well matched and rarely disagreed.

He watched, transfixed, as Ginger threw her hands about wildly and Dom flinched out of the way.

They were most definitely having a disagreement now, the rest of the group huddled off to the side to avoid becoming collateral damage.

"What the hell?" Quinten grabbed the handle of his

10

door, prepared to find out what was going on, but Darius's firm grip on his arm stopped him. Rolling his eyes, he let go and waited for the wolf to hop out on his own side and come around the back of the SUV to open the door for him.

Quinten was pretty sure it wasn't really a safety thing—he was almost positive Darius just liked how important it made Quinten look to always have someone open a door for him.

Quinten thought it made him look like an asshole, but since he didn't give a shit what anyone else thought and had agreed on waiting for Darius before exiting vehicles or buildings back when he'd caved on the sigils at his office, he made himself sit there and wait until it was opened from the outside.

As soon as he stepped out, he gave his suit jacket a few tugs and then strode forward, eyes narrowed on the arguing couple. The instincts that had made him a shit ton of money —and kept him alive all these years—were flashing a giant warning that something was very, very wrong. There was magic in the air.

And a lot of it.

"If you'd just let me get a little closer, I could—"

"*No,*" Dominic snarled at his mate and wife, and Quinten nearly stopped in shock at the tone.

He was not surprised at all when Ginger drew herself up to her full five foot five and stuck a finger in her mate's face. "Don't you snarl at me! I'm only trying to point out—"

"He's feral!" Dominic sucked in a breath at his outburst, obviously trying to calm himself down. "Sweetheart, if you'd gotten any closer, he'd have taken your face clean off."

Before she could argue again, Dominic nodded at him over her shoulder, and Ginger whipped around, relief clear on her face when she spotted Quinten. "Thank god, a voice of reason."

"Can't say I've ever been called that." He stopped a few feet away, Darius just behind him on his right, and tucked his hands in his pants pockets. "Now, someone tell me why I'm here."

"Someone left you a message," Dominic said, subtly trying to slip his hand into his mate's and frowning at the back of her head when she swatted him away.

Quinten looked down at his Italian leather loafers and sighed. "How bloody?"

"Not that kind," Ginger said, a hint of amusement in her voice. She held up a folded piece of paper. "This was stuck to the door with magic."

Quinten took the offered sheet and opened it. "Been a minute since someone passed me a note."

He heard someone snort but didn't take his focus off the words scrawled messily across the plain white paper.

Amato—

I found something of yours. You should be more careful with your things. Tsk, tsk.

I hope you're not a fan of long goodbyes.

Tiho Draža

"Who the fuck is Tiho Draža?" Quinten snapped and held up the paper. It sounded Serbian, but he knew all the players in the area. He had an agreement with the Borko crime family; he let them use the port to bring in their drugs and fake cash at a fraction of his normal fee, and they didn't try to move in on his territory and kept any others from doing it too. The patriarch—Miloš, who'd been a crusty old bastard since the day Quinten met him—had died under less-than-natural circumstances. Vlatko, his son and heir apparent to the family business, was hinting at Quinten's involvement but was smarter than to actually flat out accuse him.

But some guy named Tiho?

He was either new to the Borko family or not important enough for Quinten to remember. Either way, he couldn't imagine why the fucker was about to ruin his day.

"And what the hell does this mean?" he added, giving the paper a quick shake.

"No idea who that is," Ginger said over her shoulder, leading the way to the warehouse's door. "But I can show you the 'thing' it's referring to."

He could hear the disgust in her voice and started to get a bad feeling as he followed her into the dimly lit space. There were mountainous stacks of boxes on pallets, each one wrapped tight in plastic to keep secure and organized. A pallet truck was parked right next to the entrance, and the small office was at the far end, but the place was empty at that time in the evening, everyone having left for the day.

As they neared the back corner, a low sound that seemed to be part hiss and part growl began to grow louder, and the weight in Quinten's stomach got heavier.

He knew that sound. That was an angry feline shifter. Like, really angry.

They came around a haphazard stack of empty pallets, and Ginger held up a hand to stop him, but his feet were frozen in place anyway.

"Don't get too close," she said softly. "That just seems to agitate him more."

Quinten followed the chains bolted into the walls of each side of the corner down to where they connected to the thick leather collar around a naked man's throat.

A very attractive and very pissed naked man.

He was half crouched, but Quinten got the feeling he'd be lower if the chains allowed it, and that infuriated him for some reason. There were half-healed bruises and cuts all over his body, like he'd recently fought for his life, and he

13

saw fucking red. What the hell had happened to this guy, and how had he ended up in Quinten's warehouse?

Glowing golden eyes snagged and held Quinten's attention as the world tilted around him.

Slowly, the man pulled his lips back, baring his long, perfectly white fangs, and Quinten's dick fucking *twitched*.

What. The. Fuck.

Chapter Two

It took longer than Quinten would admit for him to realize Ginger was talking to him, gesturing expansively and clearly agitated.

"But whenever we get any closer, he... Well, he doesn't like it," she finished, and Quinten nodded along, understanding the gist even if he'd missed most of the words.

Tearing his gaze away from the shifter's hypnotizing eyes, he turned to Darius. "Do we know him?"

The wolf was scenting the air, brows furrowed, but he shook his head right away.

"What is he?" he asked, his attention sliding back to the man despite his best efforts. Not only was he healing from injuries, but Quinten could see his ribs and collarbones too well for his liking. He knew—from growing up with Liam and spending more time than was probably wise as an adult around shifters—they burned a ton of calories, especially when they changed forms. Whoever had left this guy for him hadn't been taking care of him.

"Jaguar," Darius muttered, stepping forward to get a better look with his good eye.

The man immediately pressed into the corner of the

warehouse, making a low growling sound that raised the hair on the back of Quinten's neck, but Darius ignored him. The wolf lowered himself to the cat's level and audibly inhaled.

"What is it?" Quinten asked.

"Magic," Darius grunted, easing closer still. He was within range if the jaguar decided to strike, but the filthy man just pressed back farther, eyes barely slitted open and looking like he wanted to sink into the wall. "The collar's covered in it. Or made from it."

Ginger started forward, but Dominic stopped her, grabbing her upper arm. Sighing, she didn't try and get away, just turned and met Quinten's gaze. "Maybe that's why he hasn't said anything. Maybe he can't?"

Jaw tightening, Quinten studied the feline for a long moment. Despite the grime and injuries, he truly was beautiful, his cheekbones works of art. His lips were chapped and their pinkish color dulled, but they were lush in a way that kept drawing his attention. If he were a better man, he would probably feel bad about that.

He glanced around at the small group of his men gathered behind him. "Are we *sure* we don't know him?"

Everyone shook their heads, the shifters looking a mix of pissed and curious.

"Can we remove the collar here?" he asked, turning back to Ginger. She was plucking at her lip, staring at the cat, her husband glued to her side.

"I don't think we should try," she finally said. "We could do more harm than good if I try to break it without understanding exactly what its purpose is and what it's made of."

Quinten held back a sigh. "Dare, break the fucking chains. I don't want to keep standing here. This whole situation feels..."

"Fucked-up," Dominic muttered when he didn't finish his thought.

But that worked.

Darius nodded and stepped over to a wall, reaching up to grip where the metal links were anchored. Quinten glanced back at the jaguar and got caught in his glowing stare once more. Instead of watching the wolf, his eyes were transfixed on Quinten.

He looked... surprised?

With a grunt, Darius pulled on the chain so hard the link connected to the anchor broke. A bright orange light flashed, blinding everyone for a few moments. Quinten jerked his head to the side, cursing and blinking to try and clear his vision.

A pained cry had followed the flash, but he couldn't *fucking* see.

"Dare! You okay? What happened?" he called. He was starting to get some of his sight back, but there were still spots obscuring his vision. He could see well enough a second later to realize Darius was on the ground, hands covering his face and groaning.

Quinten started toward him, his legs unsteady for some reason, but a strong grip on his shoulder stopped him. He turned his head, ready to fire someone on the spot, but the look on his man's face froze the words on his tongue. Following the younger guy's wide-eyed gaze, his whole body locked tight at the sight of the collared man writhing on the dirty floor, mouth open in a silent scream as he clawed at his own neck.

"Jesus," Quinten cursed, taking in the scene around them.

Most of the shifters in the room were still blinking and rubbing at their eyes. He glanced to his left and found Dominic with his whole body wrapped around his mate.

"Ginger, Dom, go check on Darius. Make sure he's fucking okay."

They both nodded and headed toward the wolf. Darius didn't seem to be in as much pain as he had been before, but his arms were still crossed over his eyes, and his chest was heaving as he panted. Knowing that Ginger would help him however she could, he headed for the other man.

"Sir," the wide-eyed guy behind him said, but Quinten ignored him.

He strode over to the corner of the room where the man was still writhing in pain, eyes squeezed shut and face red. There were bleeding scratches on his neck from where he'd scrambled frantically to remove the collar. Quinten's heart clenched, the sensation shocking and unfamiliar.

Following his instincts, Quinten carefully knelt next to him. "You're going to be okay," he said firmly.

At the sound of his voice, the cat's eyes popped open. That close, their glow was even more hypnotizing, sucking Quinten in and ensnaring him. He could see so much pain and fear but also curiosity, like the shifter didn't know what to make of Quinten any more than he did of him.

Slowly, he extended one of his hands, ignoring some of his men behind him warning him. The jaguar never looked away. He kept his eyes locked on Quinten's, his breaths ragged but his fingers stilling and curling into fists in front of his shoulders.

As soon as he laid his palm between the cat's pecs, he felt a shock hit his skin and travel up his arm and into his chest, tripping his heartbeat.

The jolt was so hard he fell backward, landing on his ass a couple of feet away. His heart restarted a second later, but the rhythm felt... different. Somehow. He couldn't explain it, but for a moment, it was like there was a second beat in his chest.

It was terrifying and overwhelming, but when it faded away, he missed it with an ache that throbbed behind his ribs.

By the time he climbed back onto his feet, feeling shaky and disoriented, he saw that the jaguar was unconscious, but one of his arms was extended.

In the same direction Quinten had fallen.

He stared at those outstretched fingers for a long moment and then turned and found Darius on his feet once more, Dominic and Ginger on either side of him. The wolf's face was paler than normal, but his scowl was firmly in place. He wasn't impressed with Quinten approaching the cat either.

"Don't glare at me like that," Quinten told him. "Are you good?"

Darius nodded once, but the frown on his face didn't ease at all. Suppressing the urge to roll his eyes, Quinten turned to the rest of his men.

"Get him back to headquarters—and be careful."

He forced himself to walk away without looking back. It felt like an itch between his shoulder blades, not having his eyes on the man, not making sure that he was being taken care of as gently and carefully as possible, but he forced himself to do it.

If getting out of a car after opening his own door was showing weakness, he couldn't imagine how Darius would feel if he found out Quinten was so... intrigued by the jaguar. It didn't matter anyway. Once they got the collar off him, they'd figure out who he belonged to and send him back home.

As he exited the warehouse, he ignored the way his fingers clenched at his sides, hating the idea of sending the man away.

Which was ridiculous. He didn't even know him, and Quinten had an empire to run.

"So what you're saying is you can't remove it?" Quinten asked, running a hand through his hair.

Ginger and the other witches exchanged glances, and then she finally took a step toward him. He didn't appreciate how nervous she appeared, like she was worried about giving him bad news, but he ignored it and paid attention to what she had to say.

"No. We've examined it and taken samples as best we can. We're worried if we mess with it too much, it'll hurt him again like it did before," Ginger said carefully, her eyes drifting over to where the jaguar was still unconscious.

He was laid out on a couch in one of the rooms Quinten used to meet with his inner circle. It was in the same building as his penthouse, just one floor down. He owned the whole building and had renovated the two beneath his apartment to make them one multilevel one that they used as their headquarters. He did the work for Amato Imports down at his *official* office, but all of the things that he did that weren't quite legal and had to do with the parahuman world he handled out of this one.

The jaguar had been cleaned up, and someone had put him into sweatpants that were a little too short for him, his bony ankles on display.

"So what's your suggestion?" Quinten asked, his own eyes lingering on the unconscious man.

She sighed, drawing his eyes back to her, and then shrugged helplessly. "We're not powerful enough to break the spell. You need to find more powerful witches. I'm sorry."

She sounded like it too, like it physically hurt her to disappoint him.

Standing, he walked over to her and gently clasped the left side of her neck. The other side had a faint scar from when Dom had bonded with her. He made sure to never touch that side. "You are powerful," he said, making sure she heard him. "But this is something new and complex, something you've never seen before, yes?"

She nodded. "It's definitely unlike anything I've ever seen before. It's almost like it's made from more than one kind of magic, but in such a way they enhance one another instead of lessening their effects."

He took that in, not really sure what it could mean, but he knew some witches who might. Giving her neck one more squeeze, he turned to her mate. "Dom, I need you to find out who this Tiho Draža fucker is."

Dom snarled. "Consider it done."

"If he's a part of the Serbian organization, I want you to let Miloš's useless son know that I will be taking a fifty percent cut out of their next ten shipments as repayment. Understood?"

Dom nodded and headed for the door.

Just before he reached it, Quinten said, "Oh, and if you run out of leads, I want you to use Ash."

Dominic whirled around, eyes glowing faintly. "Come on, Q. You can't mean that."

Annoyance surged through him, and he ignored the fidgeting witches behind him as he advanced on the wolf. "I do mean it, and I do not appreciate you questioning me. Use the necromancer if you need him. He has eyes and ears everywhere in this city. Whether you like it or not, I trust him."

Lips pressed firmly together, Dominic nodded and then tipped his head to the side, making himself vulnerable to

Quinten in the most basic way. A show of submission his shifters couldn't seem to help when he flexed his authority.

After Dom left, Quinten dismissed the coven, leaving only him and Darius, who hadn't said a word in hours, and the unconscious jaguar.

"Tell me what you're thinking," he said to Darius, though he was looking at the man on the couch.

"I don't like any of this," he grumbled and moved forward from where he'd been resting against the wall, keeping his attention on everything happening in the room.

"I don't like it either," Quinten said, popping out his cuff links and then rolling his sleeves up. He'd discarded his suit jacket... somewhere. He couldn't even remember, the last few hours blurring together.

"It's got to be the Serbians." Darius stopped next to Quinten so they were pressed shoulder to shoulder and turned to stare at the flesh-and-blood message Quinten had been left by some random guy he'd never even heard of.

"The name is definitely Serbian," Quinten said absently, crossing his arms over his chest. "But that doesn't automatically mean he's affiliated with the Borko family."

Darius snorted, not bothering to dignify that with a response.

"You think this Tiho is making a play to move up?" Quinten arched a brow at Darius.

The wolf shrugged. "That kind of speculation is above my pay grade," he said lowly, then jerked his head toward the door. "Who are you going to call about the collar?"

Quinten took a few steps toward the exit. "I have a few covens in mind."

Darius nodded, not responding. When Quinten reached the doorway, he paused and looked back, unable to stop himself that time. The man had been beautiful before, but now that he was clean and most of his bruises had disappeared, he was absolutely breathtaking.

He opened his mouth to tell Darius to keep an eye on him overnight and let him know if anything changed. But instead, the words "Bring him up to the penthouse" came out.

Darius turned to frown at him.

Quinten sighed. "Just do it."

He walked out before Darius could argue with him, heading down to the elevator. Darius would be right behind him, even though he disagreed with Quinten's decision. Hell, he was right to disagree with it. They went out of their way to keep Quinten safe from unknown parahumans around them, and then he went and invited one into his home, one who was injured and scared.

Not the greatest combination for a house guest, but Quinten wanted him in his space. He wanted to be able to check on him if need be, to have eyes on him. He didn't know where the urge was coming from, and it was annoying, but he also had to admit—at least to himself—that the idea of being the one to actually care for the man... warmed something inside him.

Maybe he was coming down with the flu or something.

As soon as he was upstairs, he headed straight for the master bedroom, quickly stripped, and walked into his obnoxiously large shower. The hot water hit him, and he took a deep breath, trying to relax the tension out of his shoulders and neck.

What a shit end to his day. The call from Gabriel Morde on behalf of Rick Kincaid to threaten him into complying with their new proposed rules had been bad enough, but the fact that someone thought they could come at him by using some poor parahuman who had nothing to do with him or his business was bullshit.

No one told him what to do, and no one made moves in his city without his fucking permission.

For years, he'd built up both of his businesses in his city, carving out the whole thing as his territory, and no one had bothered him. Any packs that tried to move in were unceremoniously pushed back, and any stray parahumans who didn't follow his rules were sent packing. Those who did were allowed to stay and were protected under his umbrella of control.

But now, the parahuman world was changing.

As corrupt as the shifter Council had been, they'd been stable. They'd kept a hand on the scale, sure, but that made them predictable. He could account for it and build his plans accordingly. He had learned to work with and around the Council, greasing palms and delivering extremely rare herbs to their coven free of charge as needed. He'd done whatever was necessary to make sure they stayed out of his business and territory.

And now they were gone.

Sure, he understood why Gabriel's alpha had done what he had. The Council had been targeting the Kincaid Pack, and they weren't going to stop. It was obvious to anyone who was paying attention.

But it sure was throwing a wrench into things for Quinten.

As he stepped out of the shower, he heard a noise. He quickly threw on a pair of sleep pants, grabbed another, and then followed the sound.

He found Darius pulling the covers up over the jaguar—in the guest room farthest away from Quinten's own bedroom.

There was a lamp on the floor just inside the door that used to sit on the dresser.

He gave Darius an incredulous look.

The wolf shrugged unapologetically. "Heavier than he looks."

Quinten shook his head and left the mess for the morning. "You can go home and get some rest."

Darius stared at him.

Quinten stared back.

Finally, he sighed. "You're such a mother hen. Fine. Take another guest room."

Nodding, Darius walked over and brushed their shoulders together, then headed out, probably for the room right next door.

Quinten bit back a smile. Darius scented him more than any of the other shifters he employed, and he knew part of it was because of how much time they spent together. He and Darius were as close as family, and wolves were exceptionally social.

Growing up, his brother, Liam, would sprawl against him on the couch or sneak into his bedroom to cuddle at night. When Quinten was a teenager, it had started to annoy him in the way only teenagers could be annoyed by easy affection. He'd finally asked Liam why he did it so often, and his brother had just stared at him like it was obvious and said, "So you smell like me."

He wasn't sure what that was supposed to mean, but Liam—who'd maybe been eight at the time—had just shrugged and said, "You're pack. You're supposed to smell like me and you."

To his baby brother, that was all that was important. That was the way it was supposed to be, so it didn't matter that Quinten was human and didn't need the comfort of shared scents. They were pack. Period.

He knew that was part of why Darius did it as well. To him, they were a pack, but Quinten knew that wasn't true. He was just... human. A disgustingly rich human who did things others viewed as questionable to get richer and more powerful.

Didn't exactly sound like alpha material to him.

Sighing, he moved over to the bed and carefully peeled the covers back. Without letting himself think too much about why he was doing it, he grabbed the waistband of the sweats somebody had put the jaguar in and tugged them down. He tossed them toward the corner of the room once he freed the cat's long legs from them and then gently eased them into the pair of sweats that Quinten had brought from his own bedroom.

It was harder getting them back up than the others had been to get down without the man helping by lifting his hips, and it was hard for Quinten not to look at his soft cock lying there, jostling every time he moved him.

He wasn't as morally corrupt as people thought though, so he kept his hands on task, eyes averted as much as possible, until he finally got the waistband tugged up to his hips. While that covered some of the man's body, his top half was still bared to Quinten's gaze.

He might not be completely amoral, but he was no saint either. For a few minutes, he studied the cat's torso and face. He was... distractingly beautiful. All lean muscles and white skin with just a hint of a golden hue. He wondered if the jaguar lay out in the sun naked or if it was his natural coloring.

The thought had his cock thickening, an image of all of that soft skin lounging by Quinten's pool.

Clearing his throat, Quinten tugged the blankets back up and over him.

"Where did you come from?" he murmured, stopping himself from brushing some of his hair from his brow. "How did you end up in that warehouse?"

26

And what had the note meant about Quinten being careful with his things?

This man wasn't part of his business or a member of his inner circle. He wasn't even one of the shifters that he allowed to live within the city. Even if he didn't recognize every single one on sight, Darius would have.

A thought occurring to him, he pulled out his phone and snapped a picture of the man's face, sending it to Liam.

Quinten: *Do you know this guy?*

It was late, but he wouldn't be surprised if Liam got back to him quickly. His brother didn't sleep well anymore, hadn't since becoming alpha of the Silver Oak Pack down in Kansas. He said responsibility didn't sit well on his shoulders, but Quinten got the feeling it was more than that.

There was a restlessness to his brother, like he couldn't quite get comfortable in his new home and role. Liam denied it, but Quinten had helped raise him—he knew his brother better than anyone. But he also knew Liam wouldn't tell him what was wrong until he was ready.

Quinten wasn't sure how long he stood there gazing down at the unconscious man, just watching him breathe and cataloging his long eyelashes, the curve of his lips, the sharpness of his collarbones.

He felt more than heard something behind him.

Turning, he found Darius standing in the doorway, phone in hand.

"What's wrong, Dare?"

The wolf jerked his head toward the hallway. "We've got a situation."

Chapter Three

C aden regained consciousness slowly, his mind fighting it. Not because he wanted to stay asleep but because as he crept toward being awake, pain grew through his body. The kind of strength-stealing, soul-crushing pain he'd become achingly familiar with.

He wasn't sure what had roused him at first. All he could focus on was how heavy his limbs were and how his throat felt torn apart like he'd been screaming for hours.

Goddess, he was so thirsty.

He couldn't remember what had happened after the chain to the collar broke, everything just a blur of screaming pain and fear, but he could tell by the softness beneath him and the pleasant scent teasing at his nose that he was somewhere different than that freezing warehouse.

At least he wasn't back at the Bad Place. He could tell before his eyes even opened.

There had never been anything soft or nice-smelling there.

But was he somewhere better?

Or worse?

Turning his head with a soundless whimper, he forced his eyes open and took in the bedroom he'd been sleeping in. It was completely unfamiliar but nicer than anywhere he'd ever stayed before.

He forced himself to sit up, despite his bones and muscles protesting vehemently, and caught a scent. Orange blossoms. He remembered that. He remembered that scent and worried hazel eyes. Dark hair sprinkled with silver. The way the others had turned to him for orders.

He'd been human, yet even the other shifters in the warehouse had deferred to him.

Taking a shuddery breath, Caden reached up with trembling fingers and found the collar that man had put on him, the one that wouldn't let him make a single sound and hurt like hell. Even before the chain had been broken, it radiated pain through his skin, into his muscles and bones. An endless pulsing of agony seeping into him and draining him of strength and energy.

He took another deep breath, and a little of his misery eased.

Despite everything he had been through, every pain he was feeling, the scent of orange blossoms sinking into his lungs and mixing with his blood soothed him. He knew it was probably foolish, but this place—that man—felt safe.

Slowly, he scooted over until he was sitting on the edge of the bed, panting. The bedroom he was in didn't have a lot of decorations and nothing personal that he could see, so he knew it wasn't that man's bedroom.

He tried to ignore the disappointment that shot through him.

A crumpled-up shadow in the corner caught his eyes. He stumbled to his feet and shuffled over, carefully bending and picking up a pair of sweats. He glanced down at the ones he was wearing and then back at the ones in his hand.

Lifting them to his nose, he took a quick sniff. They didn't smell like orange blossoms at all. There was a hint of wolf and magic.

Oh, that was right.

He remembered the mated pair that had been part of the group who first found him in the warehouse, the curvy little witch and her scowling mate, who wouldn't let her anywhere near him.

Which had been smart.

Caden had been out of his mind with terror and pain. He hadn't known if they were there to hurt him more or not, and he'd been trapped, chained to the wall. Naked and vulnerable. Unable to speak or shift.

If she had gotten too close, he probably would have hurt her.

He let the sweats drop back down to the floor and spotted a door that was partially ajar. He moved over to it, grateful to find a bathroom.

After relieving himself, he washed his hands and then cupped them to hold as much water as he could. He drank and drank and drank until the fire in his throat was abated.

Sighing, he leaned his hands on the counter and dropped his head. He was so tired, his brain foggy and sluggish. He should just go back to bed. It was the middle of the night. The man who smelled like orange blossoms was probably asleep somewhere in this place.

Just as he headed back to bed, he heard a thump that paused his steps, his instincts flaring. Other people were awake. He strained much harder than he should have needed to to try and catch any words being said, but it was all indistinguishable.

He made his way out of the bedroom slowly, unsure if he should hide or confront whoever was out there. In the end, he knew he wouldn't be able to go back to sleep until he was sure he and the human who lived here were safe.

He stood in the hallway outside his bedroom, trying to orient himself, and jolted hard when somebody screamed. Goose bumps shot down Caden's spine, nearly dragging him under into memories of other screaming voices, pleas for help. Begs for mercy.

Sometimes his, sometimes the others in the Bad Place.

He closed his eyes and took a few deep breaths, centering himself with the comforting scents around him. He wasn't in that place anymore. Wherever he was, it *had* to be better than where he'd been.

He made his way down the hallway, following the sounds of raised voices and the scent of blood. It was faint, but it was there, and it started riling his jaguar inside him despite the weakening effects of the collar.

Wherever he was, the place was enormous. The hallway was long and filled with multiple bedrooms, but the one he'd been put in was on the end. He crept forward and found a jaw-dropping living room that had a twelve-foot ceiling, the widest and most comfortable-looking couch he'd ever seen, an enormous TV mounted on a wall between two sets of bookshelves and over an enormous electric fireplace, and floor-to-ceiling windows taking up another wall.

He stepped closer and realized they were really high up, a whole city down below them.

It was breathtaking, but a man screaming, *"I didn't do anything, you fuckers!"* stopped him from staying there and appreciating the view.

The voice was loud and obstinate, but the scent of fear was thick in the air, tickling at the primitive parts of Caden's brain and triggering his own fear once more.

With small, reluctant steps, he made his way to the other side of the large apartment. He forced himself to keep moving, even though he desperately wanted to go back to his room and hide.

He didn't use to be this way. Sure, he was cautious as he moved from pack to pack, but he'd never doubted his ability to protect himself before.

But after months of being in that place, he could barely force himself to keep moving. He had to though. He could smell orange blossoms just beneath the blood and fear. It wasn't the man with the hazel eyes who was screaming in terror, but he was in there. He was in that room, and Caden and his jaguar couldn't leave without making sure he was okay.

He was almost there. Just a few more steps. He could do this.

The door had been left half open. As he approached, he heard that familiar deep voice, so smooth and calming. "Don't bother denying it. We know what you've been doing."

"You've got the wrong guy," the stranger said beseechingly. "Just let me go. I swear I won't tell anyone."

That was a lie.

Caden could hear it in the off-rhythm beat of his heart and smell it in the souring of his scent. Whoever that man was, he wouldn't slink off quietly.

Pressing his back to the wall, Caden carefully peered around the edge of the doorway to get a look inside. It was some sort of office. There was dark wood flooring and a small navy couch in front of floor-to-ceiling bookshelves.

He could just make out the corner of a desk, but what held his attention was the man on his knees in front of the desk. His face was swollen, blood oozing from a split lip and a cut under one of his eyes. There was a tear in his T-shirt, like someone much stronger had grabbed it and used it to move the human.

Not even a foot away were two long legs that Caden instinctively recognized, though they were clad in black sweats instead of gray slacks. The man from the warehouse must have been leaning against the front of the desk, his legs stretched out in front of him in a relaxed posture.

There was a third person in the room. Caden could clearly see the wolf who had been with the human at the warehouse standing just behind and looming over the kneeling man.

He was... scary looking.

He was enormous, both tall and broad and covered in thick, well-honed muscles. His black hair was buzzed up over his ears in a high fade, the longer bits on the top wavy. He had copper-colored skin and wore dark jeans and a plain black T-shirt.

But it was his face that sucked the breath from Caden's lungs.

He had a scar down the left side, going all the way from his hairline through one thick brow and over his eye to the corner of his mouth, pulling it into a sneer. The iris of the injured eye was cloudy and dull despite his other one glowing hotly with rage. Caden wondered if he could see out of the eye at all. He also couldn't help but wonder what had happened that had left a permanent scar on a shifter. It was so rare and usually was caused by wolfsbane being used.

He shuddered in sympathy. Having to walk through the world with a reminder of what was probably the worst thing to ever happen to the wolf had to be excruciating.

Caden quietly inhaled deeply to try and figure out what was happening, surprised when he picked up the scent of another shifter on the human. The faint smell of a rabbit was entwined with his own scent, making Caden think they were in a relationship or very close friends.

"Dare," the Orange Blossom Man said softly.

The wolf grunted in acknowledgment but didn't take his eyes off the man on the floor.

"Do we have the wrong man? Is this not Benny's boyfriend?"

The cowering man gave himself away before Dare shook his head, spiking with shock and renewed fear.

"It's him. Took him from Benny's apartment," Dare said. His voice was raspy, almost guttural.

One of the Orange Blossom Man's feet tapped on the floor twice. "Well, you see, you are who we're looking for."

"Why are you doing this? Whatever Benny said I did, he's a liar."

Caden could practically see the hackles go up on Dare. He really didn't like that answer.

Caden didn't know who this Benny guy was, but it was obvious he was important to Dare and the Orange Blossom Man. He shoved down the little spike of jealousy that shot up at the idea of *his* human caring so much about another person.

The man wasn't his. He didn't even know his name, for fuck's sake.

Nobody said anything for a moment, but those long legs moved back as the Orange Blossom Man pushed off his desk. He came fully into view, his back to Caden and blocking the man on the floor.

Caden didn't know why, but he was a little surprised to see that he was wearing a dark red silk robe. He couldn't stop himself from wondering if he was wearing a shirt underneath as he stared at his wide back. The robe's tie was hanging down at his sides, so Caden knew it was open in the front. Was he bare-chested? Were Dare and the man on the floor staring at his bare skin?

Annoyance bubbled through his veins.

35

"Do you know who I am?" the Orange Blossom Man asked, his words deceptively calm as his anger burned in Caden's nose.

"Yeah, you're his boss. The gangster. Amato."

Dare growled, but Caden barely noticed, his chest heating for some reason at the sound of the human's name. *Amato.*

Holding up a hand, Amato silenced his wolf and said, "Then you should have known better than to put your hands on him."

"I never—"

His words cut off, but Amato was still blocking his view, so Caden couldn't see what Dare had done.

"Stop lying," Amato hissed, leaning forward. "You got fucking sloppy. I saw the burn marks with my own goddamn eyes before they could heal."

Caden's stomach rolled, and he worried he would throw up all of the water he had chugged in the bathroom. Burn marks? They'd called this man Benny's boyfriend, but he'd been hurting him?

Amato stood and paced away, leaving Caden's view altogether. He kept his eyes on the man on the floor. He was watching Amato with narrowed, calculating eyes, all pretense dropping away, though his scent was still full of fear.

"So what? You and your mutt are going to scare me off, tell me to never see him again? What the fuck ever. He wasn't that good of a lay anyway. You can have him if you want him so bad." He sneered up at Amato as he came back into Caden's view as he circled around behind Dare. The man was trying to look tough, but Caden could see his trembling limbs and hear his racing heart. "I don't know why you care so much about some random camboy."

Caden barely heard the crude words, his mouth going

36

dry as he took in the furry chest under Amato's open robe, the dark hair sprinkled with silver that caught in the low lighting. There was part of a tattoo visible on his left pec, just enough for Caden to guess it was his name and some sort of symbol beneath it. There were several other black-inked tattoos running down his sternum. Runes, he'd guess, not that he knew their meaning or what they'd do.

Were there more hidden secrets under that silk robe?

Goddess, the man was beautiful. There was no denying it, nor was there any denying how scary the look on his face was as he stared down his nose at the man on the floor.

"We didn't bring you here to scare you off, no."

"Then what?" The crack in the cruel man's voice was undeniably satisfying to Caden and his jaguar.

Looking up, Amato locked eyes with Caden, freezing his breath in his lungs. He held his gaze as he said clearly, "I protect what's mine."

No sooner were the words out of his mouth than Dare's claws were slicing through the man's throat, blood arcing out and hitting Amato across the chest before Dare shoved the twitching body face-first onto the floor.

Amato glanced down at his stained skin and robe with irritation. "Always with the blood. You can never just snap their necks."

Looking like a scolded puppy, Dare ducked his head. "Apologies."

Amato waved him off, pulling a bright white handkerchief from his robe pocket and dabbing at the silk. "Forgiven. Did Benny see you take him?"

Dare shook his head, moving around the room. He pulled a large plastic sheet from somewhere and laid it on the ground next to the body, carelessly rolling him onto it. "He got called for a shoot. I'll take care of this asshole and call the cleaners."

Amato sighed and tossed the handkerchief onto the body, then slipped the robe from his shoulders and dropped it onto him as well.

Caden's mouth dried at the sight of all of that smooth, white skin dotted with tattoos, his jaguar pacing restlessly inside him. He'd been right. Across his left pec was the word *Amato* with an infinity symbol beneath it. He wondered what it meant to him that he got it permanently inked into his skin. There were a few more tattoos of runes on each of his forearms, but it was the bright red rose on his right hip, still half hidden by his sweats it sat so low, that held his attention the longest.

His gaze darted back up when he heard Amato say, "Come here, Dare."

Caden watched, transfixed and a little jealous, as the wolf closed the space between them and Amato laid one of his long-fingered hands on the side of his neck.

He was *scenting* him.

There was no other explanation for why he'd rub his palm on that spot, but why would a human do that? How'd he even know to do it?

The tension in Dare's thick back muscles relaxed, and he let out a soft breath.

"You did well," Amato said quietly.

Dare ducked his head, not saying anything, but his angry scent eased, turning sweet. Almost like... apple pie.

As soon as Amato removed his hand, Dare went back to working on the body. Caden was just about to slip away when Amato caught his eyes again and walked across the room toward him.

Caden was frozen in place as he watched his large body prowl toward him, more graceful than some shifters Caden had known. He was maybe only an inch taller, if that, yet his presence was full of strength and power, making Caden feel small in comparison.

"You should be in bed."

Caden bit his lip, wanting more than anything to be able to ask him a question, to talk to him, to tell him about what the collar was going to do.

Amato cocked his head, eyes dropping to his throat. "Can you tell me your name?"

Caden shook his head.

He nodded, having obviously expected that answer. Slowly, he reached up, his hand hovering a couple of inches from Caden's face while his hazel eyes studied him curiously.

Caden stiffened, desperately wanting the touch but also terrified of it at the same time.

Amato didn't move, but he was so close Caden could feel the heat from his palm like a phantom touch. His eyes fluttered. He wanted nothing more than to sink into that heat and let this commanding man and his wolf protect him.

"Go back to bed, kitten. We'll get something for you to write with in the morning, and you can tell me what the fuck happened to you."

Caden peeled his eyes back open and nodded, turning away without hesitation.

He wondered if what had happened to him in the Bad Place had somehow broken him. Why did he feel safer with that human gangster than he had any other time in his life since his parents died?

Why was he thinking about curling up next to him instead of running?

He could find a pack. Or go off on his own. Whatever he needed to start to get his life back together.

His fingers touched the leather of the collar. No, he

needed to stay. He didn't have time to find someone else to help him, and he needed to get it removed.

And then...

Then he'd find out if it was just circumstances or something else that was drawing him to that human.

He slipped back into bed, groaning silently at the ache in his bones and then shivering as he caught the scent of orange blossoms once again.

Just as he was drifting off to sleep, he heard Amato's smooth voice again.

I protect what's mine.

Chapter Four

If Quinten hadn't barely slept the night before and already been awake, he'd have been really pissed off when his brother called him at quarter to seven in the morning.

"Hello?" he answered, pouring his first cup of coffee.

"Hey, big bro," Liam said, his rumbly voice extra slow first thing in the morning. "So I asked around the rest of the pack as much as I could last night, and no one recognized the guy in the photo, though a few people had questions as to why I had a picture of a sleeping man on my phone, so thanks for that."

Quinten smirked and took a sip of his coffee. "He was more unconscious than sleeping," he provided.

"Yeah, I don't think that actually helps. So what's the story? Who is this guy?"

"That is the question," Quinten said, moving around his kitchen island and taking a seat on one of the stools. "He was left for me in one of our warehouses, chained to the wall and wearing some sort of magical collar that doesn't allow him to speak."

"Holy shit," Liam cursed quietly. "You don't know who left him?"

"Well, he signed the note."

"Note? There was a note left with him? What the hell kind of B-rated mystery movie are you living up there?"

Quinten ignored the extra commentary. "He left a note and signed his name to it, but I don't recognize it. And so far, no one else has either. I'm waiting to hear back from Dominic on whether he was able to dig anything up."

Liam hummed quietly and then didn't say anything for a moment, but Quinten didn't fill the silence. He didn't need to. He knew his brother was thinking, using that big brain of his to try and figure out what was going on.

"What exactly did the note say?" Liam finally asked.

"Basically, something along the lines of, 'I found something of yours. Say goodbye.'" Quinten squinted into the dark liquid in his mug, trying to remember.

He wasn't sure if Ginger had ended up with the note or someone else, but he should probably get it and see if there was something he'd missed at first glance.

"Well, that does sound kind of ominous, but only vaguely. It's not like he was left there, half-dead."

Quinten made a noise of agreement and took another sip.

"So this guy left you a chained-up man—"

"Jaguar shifter," Quinten interrupted.

"Okay," Liam said, drawing the word out. "A chained-up *jaguar shifter* in one of your warehouses wearing a magical collar, claims that he belongs to you somehow, even though you don't know who he is, and that you should say goodbye?"

Something tickled at Quinten's brain. "Actually, I think it said something about how I better not be a fan of long goodbyes."

Liam made a surprised noise. "I guess that's a little different. What condition is he in?"

"He's still sleeping," Quinten said, resisting the urge to go and check on him just like he had when he'd woken up. And when he finished getting dressed. And when he'd walked by the cracked-open door. "He was unconscious for hours yesterday and slept pretty much through the night. He was hurt, and the collar causes him pain too, I think, but he's nowhere near the verge of death or anything."

"That's good."

"I expect he'll be up soon. I'm hoping he can at least write down answers to some questions, like what his name is and who exactly he's supposed to be to me."

Liam chuffed, and Quinten couldn't help but smile, remembering the noise from when they were younger and his brother's lion was just beneath the surface, annoyed or intrigued. He had a feeling he knew which one it was this time.

"Maybe I should come up there. You don't know what you're facing or who could be behind this."

He smiled and said carefully, "Your place is with your pack now, not with me. I have plenty of people around to help me."

Liam grumbled under his breath before saying, "I suppose Darius is going out of his mind."

"What do you mean?"

"I recognized the pillowcase behind that guy's head. You have him in your penthouse." Liam sounded unimpressed. "Let me guess—Dare insisted on sleeping at your place too."

Quinten pressed his lips together to suppress a laugh. His brother could be such a little shit sometimes. "He was not happy, no, but we had a little issue to deal with late last night, and he hasn't gotten back yet."

43

"He left you alone with an unknown shifter?" Liam snapped, a touch of his lion's roar in his voice.

He didn't blame him, but Liam hadn't seen the way the cat had looked at Quinten last night or how easily he'd followed his order to return to bed.

Darius, for all his close-mouthed scowling, was the kind of overprotective only family could be. He wouldn't have left Quinten alone if he'd thought he was in true danger. His and Dare's trust and loyalty to one another came from the long-fought battles in the trenches as Quinten built his empire.

Other than his brother, there wasn't a single person on the planet he trusted more with his life, with his business, with... anything.

"He'll be back soon," Quinten said, not really responding because he wasn't sure how to explain the way they both just knew the jaguar wasn't a threat.

"I'm here," Darius said behind him, his voice barely more than a grunt, a to-go coffee cup in his hand.

"Everything settled?" he asked.

Darius nodded. "Yeah."

"My brother was surprised you left last night." Quinten couldn't help but tease, a small smile breaking free at the way Darius rolled his eyes.

He set his to-go cup down and leaned back against one of the marble counters, crossing his arms over his chest. "He was a threat when he was being threatening. He watched me kill a man on your orders and then just went back to bed because you said so."

Liam piped up from his phone. "You guys killed somebody last night?"

Quinten ignored him. "He could have been just pretending," he said to Darius, just to play devil's advocate.

He and his brother snorted at him.

44

Shifters. They trusted their senses too much, in his opinion.

Darius took a sip of his coffee. "No, that kid will be a member of our pack before too long. It's instinct."

"We don't have a pack," he said firmly.

His brother actually laughed at that.

Darius didn't respond, just kept sipping his drink.

Sighing, Quinten said into his phone, "If you're not going to contribute anything worthwhile, I'm going to hang up on you."

Liam laughed softly. "I should probably go. I've got an early morning meeting with my Enforcers and betas."

"How's the new one working out for you?" he asked, shaking his head when Darius opened the fridge and held an apple out to him.

"He's settling in. That mate of his is a piece of work," Liam said with a chuckle. "He's trying to learn as much as he can about parahumans as fast as he can and is driving half the pack crazy with all of his questions."

Quinten smiled softly. "I can relate."

When he was a kid and he found out about the parahuman world, he'd had so many questions, but he hadn't had anybody to talk to. The only parahumans he knew were Liam—who'd been a child—and his mom, and he wasn't about to ask the woman who'd broken up his parents' marriage what exactly it meant to be a shifter, or part of a pack, or if they still thought the same way when they were in their animal forms or any of the other millions of questions he'd had.

It wasn't until Liam got older that he started getting some answers. Having a little lion shifter around who felt the need to share every thought and wish and complaint with his big brother had filled in a lot of blanks.

"He'll settle in," Quinten said. "I'll see you soon."

"I'd like that," Liam said genuinely. "It's been too long."

"It definitely has. Love you, cub." He hung up in the middle of Liam's groan of indignation. He didn't care how old his brother got. He would always be a cub to him.

He set his phone down on the counter, staring at it for a long moment. He really did need to see his brother in person. Not just because it had been so long but because he was positive Liam would finally share what was bothering him once he couldn't avoid Quinten.

He was worried that Liam was unhappy leading a pack, but he was a natural alpha. Quinten had known that since they were kids. He had tried to boss Quinten around more times than he could count, and as he'd grown up, he'd taken on natural leadership positions within Quinten's dad's business.

Quinten had always known, though, that only a true pack would be fulfilling for him.

When he'd heard about a pack in Kansas, all-feline shifters with an aging, antagonistic alpha with no heir and was letting the pack stagnate, he'd nudged his brother in that direction.

Well, maybe more than nudged.

"Did you give Benny the number for that counselor?" he asked, raising his gaze and then narrowing his eyes.

Darius had a half-eaten apple in front of his face, but he was staring at nothing, head tipped back just a little in a way that let Quinten know he was scenting the air.

"What is it?"

"The kid. Something's wrong."

Quinten was up and moving before Darius finished speaking, the two of them racing through the penthouse. Darius got there first, of course, but Quinten wasn't far behind him.

As soon as he entered the bedroom, he cursed under his

breath. The jaguar had thrown off the bedding but was sweating profusely. As Quinten watched, he saw him shivering, head tossing back and forth restlessly.

"Shit. What is this?" he asked, moving toward the bed.

Darius was standing at the end, studying him, phone in hand. "I don't know. He smells like... I don't know."

Quinten jerked his head up. "He smells like what, Dare?"

Darius met his eyes. "He smells like death."

Sucking in a breath, he fisted his hands at his sides. "What the hell is that supposed to mean? He's not dead."

"No, but he's dying. Fast."

Before Quinten could ask any more questions, he had his phone pressed to his ear. He knew without having to ask that Darius was calling Ginger. He barely listened to Darius's side of the conversation, turning his focus back on the cat.

Carefully, he sat down next to him and brushed the hair back from his forehead. Unfocused eyes opened and met his gaze.

"You're going to be okay," he promised, but he wasn't sure the man could hear him, his eyes sliding back closed.

He tightened his hands, resisting the urge to either keep touching the cat or stand and throw something against the wall. One was inappropriate, and the other wouldn't help anything.

Fuck, he hated feeling helpless.

It was how he'd felt when he was a child, watching his family crumble in front of him, feeling second-class compared to something he could never be no matter how hard he tried. He'd worked a long time to never feel inferior to anyone or anything again.

But watching this cat burn away in front of him was driving him to the brink.

47

As soon as Darius came into his eyeline, he stood. "Is she coming?"

Darius nodded, worried eyes locking on the jaguar. "They're on their way up."

"Good." Quinten started for the door. "Keep your eyes on him. If anything changes, holler."

It only took a few moments for him to get to his own bedroom. He quickly stripped and then pulled on a clean suit, cursing under his breath. If Ginger and the others hadn't come up with anything, there wasn't time for him to negotiate with any of the covens or pack witches who he had alliances with.

He needed help, and he needed help now.

Luckily, there just so happened to be a powerful coven within an extremely powerful pack that owed him a favor.

But they wouldn't be pleasant about it, he was sure.

He was just finishing tying his tie when his phone alerted him to his front door opening. A few seconds later, he heard Ginger running through the penthouse. Shrugging into his suit jacket, he met her in there.

She had one hand hovering over the unconscious cat's body, her eyes squeezed shut as she mumbled under her breath. He waited impatiently for her to finish. When she squeezed her hand shut and opened her eyes to meet his, he knew he wasn't going to like what she was going to say.

"Darius is right. He's going to die if we don't do something immediately."

"Did you and the others come up with anything?" he asked, hoping for a long shot.

She shook her head, mouth twisting in regret. "I'm sorry. We worked all night, but we're just not confident in any of our hypotheses, at least not enough to risk his life on it, and that's what we'd be doing if we tried anything we came up with. We need somebody who knows more about this kind of magic."

He nodded. Yup, just his luck.

Her eyes dipped back down toward the bed. "I guess we know what the note meant now."

"What?"

"The note." She dug through the bag she had hooked across her body, sifting through the things inside until she pulled out a familiar-looking piece of paper and held it out to him. "The part about being a fan of long goodbyes? Whoever put that collar on him knew it was going to kill him fast enough that we wouldn't have a chance to help him. They know about us, Q. They know that you have witches but that we're a small coven and a lot of us are too young and inexperienced to deal with something this powerful."

"They're watching us," he said softly, taking the note from her. "That's what you're saying."

"They've been watching us probably for a while. That or he has some sort of seer with him, someone powerful who can keep an eye on us from afar, can know what we know, who we are. Our strengths and weaknesses."

"Maybe even both," Darius added. "Watch us physically and magically."

Fury began to build in the pit of Quinten's stomach. This was his city. These were his people. He didn't know who this Tiho was, but the motherfucker was going to regret the day he ever set his sights on Quinten and what was his.

"You should take that with you," she said, nodding at the note.

He raised his eyebrows. "Take it with me?"

"Wherever you take him, whatever coven you get to help, they might be able to find something. We couldn't find anything on the note."

"What were you expecting to find?"

"No," she said emphatically. "We couldn't find a trace of *anything*. We should've been able to find magical impressions at the very least of whoever pinned it to the wall of the warehouse, but there was nothing. Whoever left it there knew what they were doing, erased all traces of themselves from it. But maybe somebody with more tricks up their sleeve could have more luck."

"Okay. Anything else?" He nodded, slipping the note into the inside pocket of his suit jacket.

She dug out a small notebook and handed that over too. "This is everything that we could figure out about the collar, all the theories that we came up with last night. We wrote it all down. Hopefully, that'll give them a jumping-off point."

He took it and then stepped forward and clasped the side of her neck. "Thank you. I know you're disappointed, but you've done well."

"Do you want me to come with you?"

He shook his head. "He's not going to like it if I bring too many people. Dare will be with me. You and Dominic hold down the fort and keep searching for answers."

"Whatever you need, boss," she said with a smile. With one last look at the unconscious jaguar, she hurried from the room.

Darius stepped forward. "You're calling him, aren't you?"

Quinten sighed and pulled his phone from his pocket, not bothering to answer. He went through his contacts and found a number he'd never used before.

It only rang twice on the other end before a deep, menacing voice said, "This better be fucking good."

"Yeah," Quinten said, keeping his own tone hard and emotionless. "I'm cashing in my favor. Have your witches on standby. We'll be there in a few hours."

Chapter Five

As his helicopter passed through the warding surrounding the Kincaid Pack territory, he told his pilot to ignore Kincaid's instructions to land in a clearing in the southernmost area of the pack lands. He knew it was the farthest spot possible for them to be from where Rick lived with his family and he conducted business, but Quinten wasn't going to waste time moving the jaguar on the ground.

Less than ninety seconds later, they were circling the large house and landing just outside the gates.

An SUV came flying up the driveway from the main road, and he was unsurprised to see Rick Kincaid stepping out of the passenger seat before it fully stopped. Two witches, one male and one female, both with dark skin, hurried out of the back but stopped when Rick raised his hand to them, stomping toward the helicopter.

He left his pilot, Arnold, to continue shutting down and allowed Darius to pull open the door and jump out first before exiting himself.

Rick's face was thunderous as he came right toward

him, only stopping when Darius growled in warning. "I told you where to meet us."

"Yes, but I ignored you," Quinten said, gesturing toward the house. "This is where you'll be treating him."

Rick was already shaking his head. "You're not coming into my house, Amato. We'll treat him at the clinic."

Quinten took a step forward, meeting the alpha's hard stare. The base of his head prickled with instincts to look away, to avert his gaze, but he refused. He refused to show any sort of weakness or submission to this man. He didn't care that he was basically the most powerful alpha on the continent.

Quinten bowed his head to no one.

"No, you'll treat him here. It's the most secure location in your territory."

"Yes, because my family is in there," Rick snarled.

"We either treat him in there, or I get a dozen more of my men to meet us here to secure another location. I assumed you wouldn't want that many in your territory."

"You can't come in here making demands," Rick said. "This is a favor."

"No," Quinten said, losing a little bit of his pretend calm, his hands squeezing into fists at his sides. "This is repayment for me saving your goddamn life. In case you've forgotten, you owe me. So, you're going to save that jaguar, and you're going to do it in your fucking house like you would any other important guest, and then we're going to leave, and we'll be square."

He could practically hear Rick grinding his teeth as he looked from him and Darius into the helicopter and back.

"We're wasting time here, Kincaid."

Grumbling under his breath, he waved a hand, and the two witches came running. The driver of the SUV, a blonde woman with curly hair, stayed near the front of the vehicle, but she was eyeing them all carefully.

"Call Doc, tell him to get his ass over here," Rick called over to her.

She nodded and pulled out her phone.

Rick turned back to Quinten. "If you make me regret this…"

Quinten rolled his eyes. "What exactly do you think I'm going to do? Use this opportunity to rob you? Kill you? Take over your pack?"

"There's no telling what someone like you could do," Rick said quietly. "Bring him inside."

Quinten ignored the slight of his character and nodded toward Darius. He knew the wolf didn't like it, didn't want to have his hands full in case he needed to fight, but he wasn't trusting anybody else to carry the cat.

His pilot, a sixty-year-old human who'd served in the Air Force, would be staying with the helicopter while they were inside, making sure nobody tampered with it or planted a tracker.

What could he say? Rick wasn't the only one with trust issues.

He followed close behind Darius, the witches on either side muttering to each other as they looked the cat over. Their faces were grim.

He pulled out his phone and shot a text message to Ginger and Dominic, letting them know they'd arrived and to keep an ear open in case he had to call them to bring in the cavalry.

He didn't think Rick or his pack would be a problem—they were a bunch of do-gooders, after all—but overprotective alphas could be unpredictable, and the man had an army at his disposal. One that had taken down the Council, which should have been an impossible feat.

As soon as they walked through the front door, he saw Gabriel. It seemed like days ago that he'd talked to him on the phone, not a little over twelve hours. The conversation—and his anger over it—came flooding back as soon as he locked eyes on the long-haired hunter.

Well, ex-hunter.

Supposedly, he was retired, but considering some of the things Quinten had heard Gabriel and other retired hunters were doing for Kincaid, he wouldn't bet his fortune on it.

Gabriel nodded warily at him as he approached, but Darius stepped between them, a low growl coming out of him.

"Easy, Dare," he said softly, placing a hand on his shoulder. "We're all friends here, right?"

Rick grunted, walking across the entrance hall toward where a younger man with short blond hair waited for him, hands twisting in front of him.

"I wouldn't go that far," Gabriel said with a small, forced smile. "But as long as you and your wolf behave, everything should go fine."

Darius snarled at being called Quinten's, but he didn't take offense. The way Gabriel had said it had been condescending.

Quinten glanced around the large entrance hall, taking in the expensive but not ostentatious decorations and the surprising lack of people. He would've thought with a pack as big as Rick's there would have been Enforcers and betas busy at work, as well as assorted pack members running the household or coming by for help.

He glanced at Gabriel again. "It's pretty quiet around here."

Gabriel just shrugged, shoving his hands into the pockets of his cargo pants. He was wearing a hooded sweatshirt, despite the mild spring weather they were having, showing his thinner Southern blood. His long hair was down around his shoulders, the small braid with purple beads denoting his hunter clan allegiance showing.

Quinten couldn't see them, but he also knew there were bonding bite scars on each side of his neck, one from each of his shifter mates.

Gabe opened his mouth but snapped it shut when Rick started striding toward them.

"Jamie says there's an empty room on the second floor." Rick glanced at him and Darius. "We'll take him from here. You two wait with Ericka in the—"

Quinten didn't wait to hear where he thought the two of them could be hidden away to make Rick and the others feel more comfortable. "We're not waiting anywhere. Where he goes—" He pointed to the unconscious jaguar. "—we go."

Rick bared his teeth. "That's out of the question. I don't want you any closer to my family than absolutely necessary."

"I don't give a shit. A life for a life, Rick. I'm not leaving a person I'm responsible for alone with strangers who are going to be conducting magic on him. Get your witches, get your doctor, and let's go."

Rick stepped closer, his eyes flashing bright for a second before he locked himself down, but his voice still came out in a low rumble. "Watch it, Amato. I may owe you for saving my life, but you're still a fucking guest in my house."

He could feel Darius vibrating with tension, one word from Quinten away from launching himself at the alpha. But that wasn't what Quinten wanted.

Not today anyway.

"Agreed. So why don't you treat me with the courtesy you would treat any other guest in your house?" Quinten said, holding the alpha's stare once more.

The female witch stepped forward, hands on her full hips. "We really don't have time for this. I want to get him upstairs and start looking over this collar. I don't like what I'm getting off it just standing here." She ran her dark eyes over the cat's limp body, bright red lips pressed together.

Quinten glanced at her and then back at Rick before slowly unbuttoning his suit jacket and reaching inside to pull out the journal. He noticed that everyone but Darius tensed as his hand disappeared inside his jacket, but he ignored it, quietly amused that so many powerful people were so scared of him.

He held out the notebook to her. "This is what my witches have discovered and some of the theories they came up with. Hopefully, it'll help."

She looked more than a little surprised, staring down at it. "Thank you," she said quickly and grabbed it from him. She tucked the journal under one arm and extended her right. "This will be incredibly useful. I'm Tashmica Torres, by the way."

Quinten ignored the hard looks he was getting from Rick, Gabriel, and the blonde woman he assumed was Ericka and stepped forward, shaking it. "Pleasure, ma'am. Quinten Amato."

She laughed. "Yes, I've heard."

He didn't respond, turning to the other witch, who had stepped forward as well.

"Keegan Toussaint." He stuck out his hand, eyes hard.

Quinten had to wonder if he was just doing it to prove he wasn't scared of Quinten. "I've heard of both of you, of course. It truly is an honor to meet you."

Again with the looks of surprise.

Quinten ignored them, stepping back next to Darius and glancing expectantly at Rick. "Shall we proceed?"

Jaw tensing, Rick led the way up the stairs, Gabriel trailing behind their group.

They went down several hallways before stopping outside a bedroom with the door open. The bed inside was large and freshly made, the curtains open to show the bright blue sky outside.

"Lay him there," Rick said, gesturing at the bed.

Darius rolled his eyes but did it, stepping back to plant himself just behind Quinten as soon as his arms were free.

Tashmica and Keegan ignored the bubbling testosterone, hurrying forward to take a closer look. Quinten could tell right away that they worked together often. They used a sort of shorthand with each other, barely saying more than a few words before the other either shook their head or nodded.

Tashmica opened the journal and started quickly reading through it, pointing out certain things to Keegan as she went or shaking her head and turning the page when she found something she didn't agree with. It was fascinating but also frustrating as he was forced to stand there and do nothing but wait.

He knew they had to first figure out what kind of spell had been used to create the collar and then figure out how to break it. But there wasn't much time. As he stood there, the jaguar's face grew paler and paler.

He didn't realize how much of his focus was on the man lying on the bed until he felt Darius shift next to him, and he glanced over and saw a pair of men, one large and white, the other a much smaller Latino.

"What have we got, Tash?" the big guy said, moving straight for the bed and not even acknowledging Quinten or Darius.

The smaller man gave them both wary glances but kept close to the other. An instinct honed from being surrounded by parahumans for most of his life told him the two were mated.

"We're not quite sure yet," Tashmica said. She had the notebook sitting on the bedside table, open on a specific page, so that both of her hands could be free as she worked with Keegan. "We're pretty sure it's a variation of the Consumption Spell."

"Jesus Christ," Rick muttered, running a hand through his hair.

Quinten glanced at him, but when he didn't say anything else, he turned back to the witches. "What does that mean?"

"It means the spell works like a parasite, feeding on his magic," she said, not looking up.

"His magic?" Quinten asked.

"His jaguar," Darius said lowly.

Well, that didn't sound fucking good.

Quinten stepped up next to the bed. "But you can stop it by removing the collar, right? And then he'll heal."

"In theory," Keegan said. "We've had to do something like this before," he added tentatively.

"Okay." Quinten glanced among the witches. "And that person survived?"

"I did," Rick said, crossing his arms over his chest. He was acting unbothered, but Quinten noticed his skin looked paler and his eyes were locked on the jaguar in a way they hadn't been before.

"It almost killed him first though," the big guy said, stethoscope in his ears. "He was a lot further along by the time we were able to get him help than this guy seems to be. That, or it's a much weaker variation of the spell." He glanced at Tashmica. "Which would make sense. The version used on Rick was done by an extremely powerful coven."

She nodded, pulling out her phone and starting to type a message. "Agreed. Plus, he's not as strong as Rick is. It doesn't have as much fuel for the spell, so it's moving slower. That's to his advantage," she added, glancing at Quinten like he would think that was an insult.

As far as he was concerned, he didn't care if the cat was the weakest shifter known to man. He just needed him to survive. He wasn't quite sure why he cared so damn much, but he did. Them meeting in the warehouse might have been orchestrated by Tiho Draža, but it felt... inevitable.

There was no way he was leaving Kincaid's territory without him.

"So what do you need to do?" he asked.

"Concentrate," the little guy next to the doctor said, shooting an apologetic smile toward him and Darius. "We need to concentrate. Anyone who isn't needed in here should leave."

"I am not going anywhere." He turned to the silent wolf next to him. "He's right though. Wait in the hall, Dare."

Darius curled his lip in a silent snarl but didn't protest. He waited just inside the room, though, until Gabriel put his hands up in surrender and walked out too. Rick stayed, but it wasn't like anyone could tell him in his own house to get the hell out. The Enforcer, Ericka, had slipped away not long after the doctor and his mate showed up.

Hours passed.

The witches and the doctor worked together. He assumed they were making progress since the cat wasn't dead yet, but the magic stuff went right over his head.

Rick left at one point and then came back a while later, silently holding a bottle of water out to Quinten. Now, he was posted up against the wall just inside the room, eyes on the bed.

Quinten hadn't moved except to take tiny sips of the

59

water. His eyes were getting scratchy because he kept forgetting to blink, and his low back was killing him, but still, he didn't move.

The sun was starting to set when a soft knock came to the ajar door. Quinten glanced over, his eyes stinging and bleary. He recognized the man standing in the doorway. Tall, shaved head, dark brown skin—that was Rick's second-in-command, Bennett Young.

He was surprised to see a small child in his arms though.

The baby had alabaster skin and was maybe eight or nine months old. It was hard to tell. Quinten wasn't that familiar with kids. Plus, anything looked tiny next to the giant second. The baby was passed out, mouth gaping, and his bald little head tucked up underneath the tiger's chin.

Bennett glanced at the bed and then Quinten before turning to Rick and saying something too quietly for him to hear. Rick nodded and followed him out of the room, not giving a second glance to Quinten. He supposed after all these hours of him not going berserk and trying to murder them all meant he'd been deemed not much of a threat anymore.

More hours passed.

The world outside the windows was pitch-black. Quinten had finally been forced to move his vigil to a chair a few hours before, though he'd pulled it up next to the bed.

He was so used to letting the others' voices flow over him that he almost missed when something changed.

Over the course of the day, people had popped in carrying different things like spell ingredients and books, crystals, mortars, and pestles. It was always about fifteen minutes after Tashmica picked up her phone. He'd stopped keeping track of who was coming and going hours ago.

60

But now, the air around him had tensed, the energy shifting.

He brought his focus up to where Tashmica, Keegan, and the other guy, whose name he'd learned was Damien, and a few others he recognized from throughout the day all stood around the bed, arms held out in front of them over the jaguar's body.

Carter, the doctor, was standing off to the side, but he didn't look concerned, so Quinten took that as reassurance. The witches began to slowly chant, the lights in the room flickering and then dimming, and Quinten pushed to his feet and stepped back to make more room.

The chanting continued, all of their eyes tightly closed and brows furrowed with concentration.

There was a stirring along the back of his neck, almost like a light breeze or a gentle touch, but he knew there wasn't anything there. It was just the magic moving through the air, surrounding them.

As the words came to a crescendo, the cat was consumed by a bright, white light that forced him to look away, cursing as his eyes stung. When he could see again, he found Tashmica's grinning face right in front of him, her hand held up between them and the pieces of the collar draped over it.

"Voilà," she said, her voice hoarse and strained with exhaustion and probably dehydration. He hadn't seen any of them take a break in hours. "One uncollared jaguar."

"And he'll heal?" he asked, stepping around her to get closer to the bed. He sat just on the edge, facing the unconscious man.

"He'll heal," she said softly somewhere behind him. "It'll take a little time, and he'll need plenty of rest and quiet. Nothing too strenuous for at least the first three or four days."

"No shifting," Doc added, his voice firm. "He's going to wake up feeling a thousand times better, but he needs to let himself and his jaguar heal. So no shifting for at least a week."

Quinten nodded, reaching out and running his fingers along the inside of the cat's closest forearm. The skin was so soft. "No shifting one week, three to four days of nothing but rest. Got it. We'll make sure he follows the orders."

A light hand landed on his shoulder, drawing his attention.

"When you find who did this to him," Tashmica said, her tone hardening, "you let us know if there's anything we can do to help."

He met her eyes, a feeling of understanding passing between them, and then nodded. "You got it."

Chapter Six

Caden slowly swam into consciousness.

His body felt heavy, and his head was throbbing, but the intense pain in his muscles and bones was gone. There was a bit of ache in his joints, he discovered as he flexed his wrists and ankles, but the last thing he remembered was he'd been pretty sure he was dying, so he'd take it.

He'd barely been able to feel his jaguar, his whole body in excruciating pain, like a fire was burning through his veins, destroying everything it came into contact with. He shuddered just remembering. There were flickers of other things—words he didn't understand, scents he didn't recognize, but through it all, the comfort of orange blossoms.

"I think he's waking up," a strange voice said, and he instinctively flinched away from it.

His lids felt too heavy, and he panicked for a moment when he couldn't open his eyes.

A large, callus-rough hand cupped his cheek. He inhaled, and his entire body relaxed. He knew that person.

"Can you open your eyes?" Amato asked.

For him, Caden tried harder, forcing his eyes to slit

open and seeing the worry-lined face above him. The stern angle of his brows would have worried him if not for the soft smile gracing his tempting lips.

Butterflies exploded in his belly, and he pressed his cheek harder against Amato's palm.

"How are you feeling?" Amato asked, brushing his thumb against Caden's cheekbone and leaving a trail of tingles behind.

"Better," he croaked out, his eyes widening as he grabbed at his throat. The collar was gone. He squeezed his eyes shut, holding back tears.

It was gone. It wouldn't kill him.

"Better is good," Amato said.

"Are you in any pain?" another man asked, stepping toward the bed and finally drawing his eyes away from Amato so he noticed there were others in the room.

The guy who'd asked was huge, easily six foot five, and built broad. There was a dark-skinned woman with kind eyes and loose curls who smelled like magic so strongly it tickled his nose. But his eyes were pulled to the man standing at the far side of the room, watching him impassively, another shifter who had to be his mate right next to him, looking worried.

Even without anyone telling him, he'd know that man was a powerful alpha. He could feel it radiating off him just standing there, unmoving.

He forced himself to look at the man next to the bed who'd asked about his pain. His nose told him he was a bear, and he'd guessed he was a doctor based on the slight scent of antiseptic on him.

"A little," he admitted. He looked back at Amato, unable to keep his eyes off him. "It's a lot better though."

The doctor nodded and leaned down to rifle through

something, coming up with a syringe. "I can give you something."

The sight of the needle primed to fill him with some unknown medicine had Caden recoiling, scrambling back across the bed until Amato was between him and the danger.

"Whoa. Easy, kitten," Amato said, wrapping an arm around Caden as he teetered at the edge of the bed. "You don't have to take anything you don't want." His voice harder, he turned to the doctor. "Step back. Now."

He forced himself to look away from the needle. "Promise?"

Amato's jaw tensed, his scent spiking with anger and outrage, but Caden knew it wasn't aimed at him. "Yes, I promise."

When Caden glanced back over, the doctor had moved back, practically pressed against the wall, and the needle was nowhere in sight, his hands hanging loosely at his sides. "You don't have to take anything," he echoed Amato. "I just thought I could make you more comfortable, but I don't have to do that."

Caden nodded slowly, easing back toward the head of the bed so he could lean against the headboard. The sudden movement and terror leached what little energy he'd woken up with, leaving him heavy-limbed and lethargic.

"What's your name?" Amato asked, and Caden stared at him in shock.

It seemed so strange that he didn't know his name. Then again, Caden didn't know Amato's first name either, and yet he felt connected to him in a way he never had before... and safe.

His instincts had known what he needed when the sight of that syringe had terrified him so much, trusting the only non-magical human in the room to protect him. It made little sense, but he was too tired to argue with his own instincts.

"Caden," he said.

"Caden," the man repeated, his chin dipping in acknowledgment. He pressed a hand to his own chest. "I'm Quinten Amato."

"It's nice to meet you... officially," Caden said with a small smile.

Quinten's lips twitched too, but he sobered as another voice spoke from the other side of the room.

"Caden, we need you to tell us what happened to you."

He forced himself to turn and meet the eyes of the most powerful shifter he'd ever met. The power and authority seeping out of him was almost choking in its intensity, filling up all of the space in the room. Oppressive. Pushing in at all sides now that he was focused on him and not distracted by Quinten.

There was a hardness in his face and tenseness in his body that put Caden on edge.

Right before he opened his mouth, he made a decision.

"I... I don't remember," he murmured, stammering over the lie.

The alpha frowned and crossed his arms over his chest. Before he could say anything, the slight man next to him placed a hand on his bicep and quickly shook his head. He then turned to Caden and said, "That's alright. You've been through a lot. Rick and I are just worried about you."

Caden wasn't sure that the alpha—Rick—was all that worried about him, personally, and more suspicious of the kind of trouble Caden could bring to his pack.

He didn't begrudge him that though.

He'd been part of many packs during his life, and there were always certain things that were the same, and an alpha's protectiveness was one of them.

"I'm sorry I can't help," Caden said, drawing his knees up to his chest and wrapping his arms around them.

"Don't worry about that." Quinten placed a hand on one of his knees and gave it a squeeze. "All you need to focus on is healing and getting stronger."

Caden nodded and dropped his eyes. He didn't want to talk about what had happened to him, and there were some parts he truly didn't understand, like what had led to him being in that warehouse. But he definitely did not want to talk about the terrible things that happened in front of a bunch of people he didn't know or trust.

"Amato," Rick said, dropping his arms, "come with me. There's a few things we need to discuss."

Annoyance wafted off Quinten, but his face didn't show it, and Caden was impressed with his control.

Standing, Quinten gave the ends of his suit jacket sleeves a quick tug, nodded at Caden, and then pivoted and followed Rick out of the room.

The man who had to be Rick's mate stayed behind. He heard Quinten say to someone out in the hallway, "Stay with him," and the wolf, Dare, stepped just inside the bedroom, folding his hands in front of him.

The big bear shuffled his feet and said gently, "My name's Carter, but everyone calls me Doc. I know I freaked you out with the needles, but if you need anything while you're here, please don't hesitate to ask for me."

Caden nodded, even though he had zero intention of requesting the help of some doctor he didn't know. The man left, taking his bag with him.

Rick's mate was slight, with unruly brown hair and bright green eyes. He smiled at Caden widely, then glanced at Dare and said, "Would you mind giving us some privacy?"

The wolf shook his head. "No."

That was all he said. *No.*

Caden had to slap a hand over his mouth to suppress a laugh at Rick's mate's disgruntled face. He kind of appreciated the fact that Dare didn't even pretend to feel bad about it or explain. The other man was a shifter, so there was no way he hadn't heard Quinten ask Dare to stay with him. It seemed rude to ask him to leave after that, like he didn't respect Quinten enough to be considerate of his wishes.

He was also super grateful that Dare wasn't leaving him alone with the guy while he was so weak.

Sighing, the man came over, pulling a chair with him and sitting next to the bed. "My name's Kai. I'm the alpha-mate of this pack."

Caden bowed his head in acknowledgment and respect for his position, wondering what a man like this could want from him.

"What pack is that?" he asked, unsure where they were.

"Oh, right. Sorry," Kai said, smiling. His face was so bright and open that it automatically put Caden at ease, even though he wanted to stay alert. "You're in the Kincaid Pack territory."

Caden's spine straightened a little, surprise filling him. He'd heard of the Kincaid Pack. Of course he had. Who hadn't in the last year? He glanced at Dare, who gave him a quick nod.

"Oh" was all Caden could think to say.

"Quinten brought you here so our witches could help you," Kai added, his mouth twisting a little around Quinten's name.

All of the easiness he'd been feeling evaporated. Despite barely being able to feel his jaguar, he and his cat were immediately on the defensive.

"Well, please tell your coven thank you from me," Caden said, doing his best to keep his tone respectful.

"Of course, we were glad to help." Kai smiled again, glancing at Dare once more before scooting forward on his seat until he was right on the edge. He reached out to touch Caden's arm, but he jerked it back without thinking. Out of the corner of his eye, he saw Dare take a step forward. Kai cleared his throat and drew his hand back. "I talked to Rick earlier, and I wanted to let you know that if you'd like to stay here, you are more than welcome."

Dare growled softly, but Caden kept his eyes on the alpha-mate in front of him. Stay there? Why would he want to stay there?

"You mean join your pack?" he asked, just to make sure he was understanding correctly.

"Yes, if you'd like to." Kai's face softened. "I'm guessing that... whatever happened that led you to that warehouse and a collar around your neck that nearly killed you, you probably don't have a pack out there looking for you."

Caden flinched. That was mostly true, though he couldn't say for certain. The last pack he'd been with, he hadn't technically been a member, and he doubted anyone other than the alpha knew he was taken and hadn't just left. But the last thing he wanted was to see that alpha again.

"Living without a pack can be hard and stressful, and it can weaken you. Slow your recovery," Kai said, his words straightforward but tone gentle. "We just wanted to let you know that you have the option to stay here, if you'd like."

"If I'd like," Caden repeated, running his tongue over his dry lips. "You mean, instead of going home with Quinten?"

Kai's eyes widened, and he glanced over at Dare. "Quinten isn't part of a pack. You wouldn't have that support if you went with him and stayed in his territory."

That didn't make sense to Caden. The way that Dare

trusted him and turned to him... He would've sworn that Quinten was an alpha, even without being a shifter.

He glanced at Dare. "You don't mind living there, right?"

He shook his head, glaring at Kai. "No, I don't mind."

Kai ignored Dare, his scent turning frustrated. "You don't have to make a decision right now. For now, all you need to focus on is resting and getting stronger. We can talk again later if you want."

Caden nodded stiffly. "Sure. Later."

Kai chewed on his bottom lip as he pushed to his feet, looking like he wanted to stay and try to persuade him more, but gave one more frustrated glance toward the wolf in the corner of the room. Giving up, he told Caden to rest one more time before walking out.

He wanted to rest. Truly. His body was weighted down with exhaustion like he hadn't slept in a decade, but there was something more important he needed to do first.

Slowly, he climbed out of the bed, holding a hand up to stop Dare when he stepped forward to help.

"You should stay in bed," Dare said slowly, obviously not wanting to order Caden, just strongly suggest it.

"I'll get back in bed when we get home."

The word slipped out of his mouth without thought. He didn't know how he could think about Quinten's apartment as home when he'd barely been conscious when he was there. He stilled as he took a step forward, his bare feet digging into the plush carpeting.

It wasn't the apartment.

It was Quinten.

The realization loosened something in his chest, but he shook off the sensation. He'd think about that later. At the moment, he needed to make sure Rick wasn't bullying his human into making him stay.

He padded carefully out of the bedroom, ignoring the wolf as he followed behind him at a respectful distance, using his nose to follow the scent of orange blossoms. As he neared the room where the two of them were, he could hear them talking through the closed door.

"You're just being stubborn," Rick snarled. "That, or you really aren't as smart as they say you are."

Caden's hackles rose at the insult.

"Neither, but I'm not leaving here without everything I brought," Quinten said firmly.

Warmth pooled in the bottom of Caden's belly, his hands moving to cover the bare skin over the spot. He was one of the things that Quinten had brought and wouldn't leave without.

He was right though. Rick was trying to convince him to leave him behind.

He hovered outside the door, knowing that Rick probably knew he was there, and Dare was watching him with an almost amused look on his scarred face as Caden eavesdropped blatantly.

"He needs to heal and recover," Rick said, his voice strengthening and waning in a way that made Caden think he was pacing. "He needs a pack to do that, not whatever it is you have."

Quinten's anger billowed out from around the door, hitting Caden straight in the face, sinking into his bones, firing up his weakened jaguar.

"Whatever I have," Quinten said slowly, "has been perfectly fine for all the shifters in my territory for years."

"This is different," Rick said, scoffing. "The kind of magic that was used on him, it drained him, nearly severed his connection to his jaguar. He needs a strong bond to a strong alpha to fully recover that."

Caden felt weak-kneed for a moment. Was that what

had happened? Had he almost lost half of himself? Why? Why would anyone do something like that to him?

He expected to hear Quinten continuing to argue, but instead, there was a very soft sigh.

"You're saying if he goes with me, he might not fully recover," Quinten said, just the barest hint of a question in his voice.

Caden heard leather creak as someone sat down, and Rick said earnestly, "That's exactly what I'm saying. If you want to give him the best chance to get back to one hundred percent, then you need to do this. You need to let him go, Quinten."

Something tore at the inside of Caden's chest when Quinten didn't say anything, didn't argue, didn't fight. Unable to hold himself back, he gripped the door handle and ripped the door open.

Rick didn't look surprised at all, but Quinten's scent spiked.

Caden didn't care. He didn't care that this man was a human, that he could never be as strong, or fast, or have the kind of senses that shifters did. He truly did not care.

All he cared about was the fact that he had never felt more vulnerable in his entire life, and the idea of being left behind in a pack full of people he didn't know terrified him. He didn't know what would happen in the future. He didn't know if he would heal all the way or if his jaguar would always be weak. But he would rather risk that than be separated from Quinten.

Stumbling into the room, he went straight for his human and dropped to his knees next to him, resting his forehead on his warm thigh. The scent of shock filled the room from both men.

"Please," he begged softly. "Please don't leave me behind. Take me with you. I want to go home."

No one moved or said anything for a long moment. Quinten's whole body seemed to be frozen, but then gentle fingers stroked through his hair, and Caden almost started purring.

"Well," Quinten said thickly. "That's decided, then."

Chapter Seven

He wanted them to leave right away.

It wasn't that he wasn't grateful for the Kincaid Pack for saving his life. He just didn't feel comfortable there. He was exhausted and weak in a way he'd never been before. He wanted to curl up in a safe place and allow himself to heal, but that wasn't going to be in a bedroom in Rick Kincaid's house.

Unfortunately, the big alpha insisted they stay at least one night so his witches could check him over in the morning to make sure he really was on the mend.

Caden had to wonder if he had suggested it because he truly felt that way or if his mate had pressured him to do it, wanting another chance to try and make Caden stay.

Either way, Quinten agreed, so Caden went along with it too.

Quinten and Dare escorted him back to the bedroom he'd been given, and he yawned just as he was opening the door.

"Get some rest," Quinten said. "We'll leave first thing in the morning."

He whipped around and stared. "You're not staying?"

Quinten's scent fluctuated a little, but all he did was give a slight smile. "I need to make a few phone calls and arrangements, but they'll be putting me in the room right next door." He nodded toward a door that seemed awfully far away from his own. "And Dare will be outside your door the whole time. If you need anything, just call for him."

Caden wrapped his arms around himself, rubbing at the exposed skin and not liking this plan at all, but he didn't want to seem overly needy. After the spectacle he'd made of himself in the sitting room, he should probably conserve some of his dignity.

But he had been hoping that even if Quinten wouldn't lie down with him, he would at least stay in the room, filling it with his orange blossom scent and sense of safety so Caden could actually rest. He didn't say any of that though. He just pasted on a smile and stepped into the bedroom, letting it drop when Quinten closed the door for him.

He did end up falling asleep for a while, but when he woke up, the clock on the wall told him that it was still the middle of the night. He sighed, turning on his side.

There was a pitcher of water and a covered plate on the bedside table. He wondered if Dare or Quinten had brought it in, knowing if it had been anyone else, he would have woken up as soon as the door opened.

He drank two glasses and then ate the burger that was still sort of warm. Both made him feel a little more like normal. His body didn't ache as much, but he could still barely feel his jaguar inside him, and his cat was quieter than he'd ever been. He told himself not to panic, that he was already feeling better, and it had only been half a day. He needed to give himself time.

Tiptoeing, he went over and cracked open the door. Dare was standing right there, waiting for him, scarred eyebrow raised in question.

Maybe one day, he'd know him well enough to ask about the scar. As a shifter, he should have healed, even if his eye had been too damaged to repair itself.

"Alright?" the wolf asked, his voice quiet and rumbly. "Bathroom?"

Dare nodded. "Three doors down."

Caden slipped out of his room and headed that way. Quickly, he relieved himself and then washed up. There were extra washcloths and toiletries sitting on the counter, so he made use of them to clean his face and his body a bit. He couldn't remember the last time he'd showered and shuddered. In the morning, he'd ask Dare or Quinten for new clothes so he could.

He wondered if Quinten had been the one to wash him up at his penthouse, his blood heating at the idea.

As soon as he finished, he crept back down the hallway, gave Dare a grateful smile, and went back inside. He lay down, but he wasn't feeling overly tired anymore, and even though the house was well-built to reduce the amount of noise, there was enough that it kept snagging at him, drawing his attention and keeping him wide-awake.

He tossed and turned for a while before flopping on his back and staring up at the ceiling.

There were still five hours before he could politely get up and request that they leave, and that was going to feel like an eternity if he was awake the entire time and didn't have something to do other than let his mind run over all of the things that had happened to him recently.

Not the good things, like meeting Quinten.

The bad things. The things he tried not to think about.

His whole body jerked when there was a soft knock on the door. His nose told him it was Dare before it opened and the wolf's head appeared.

"Can't sleep?"

Caden sat up on his elbows and shook his head. "No, it's too... I don't know. I can't get comfortable though."

Dare nodded and came all the way inside, something black and square in his hand. "Yeah, I can't sleep somewhere I don't feel safe either."

Caden was pretty sure that was the longest sentence the wolf had ever said to him, and he also really appreciated what he was doing, letting Caden know that he wasn't being ridiculous.

Dare came over and held out the object he was holding. It was a tablet of some sort, the screen off.

"I got this for you."

"You 'got it'?" Caden asked, smiling a little and running his fingers over the edges of the device.

Dare tipped his head to the side. "Borrowed it."

Caden decided not to ask if the owner knew that it had been borrowed and simply murmured a quick thank-you.

"It's already hooked up to the Wi-Fi. You can watch something."

That got Caden's attention, his excitement spiking. Goddess. When was the last time he'd been able to watch something just for fun? Just to relax and turn his brain off?

He expressed his gratitude again as he clicked it on and started going through the apps, picking one and then a sitcom he'd heard about but never had a chance to watch. He was settling in, his back propped up against the pillows and the tablet on his raised legs, when he realized that Dare had settled into a chair in the corner.

"Do you want to come watch?" Caden pointed toward all of the empty space next to him.

Dare shook his head. "Can't. Go ahead and relax."

Caden nibbled on his lip, wanting to ask why he couldn't. He wondered if that was just an excuse and what he'd meant was he didn't *want* to. He didn't *want* to be that close. He didn't *want* to share scents like pack mates.

He tried not to take it personally. Just because Caden was feeling connected to Quinten and his people and would've found comfort in the wolf's closeness didn't mean Dare felt the same way. Sharing space, scents, and comfort like that was usually reserved for pack, and they weren't that.

No matter how much he wished otherwise.

No matter how much he wished he could just sink into the safety of Quinten and Dare's pack and never leave.

Instead, he watched the show by himself, the only company in the room a silent wolf with a scarred face, who'd at least come inside to offer what he could.

He wasn't sure when he fell back asleep, but when he woke again, the tablet was sitting on the bedside table and the sun coming in through the windows. The chair that Dare had been sitting in was empty. He rubbed at his eyes and ignored the way his cheeks were heating.

Even on the other side of the room, Dare had been close enough to help settle Caden's restless jaguar and allow him to sleep, knowing that someone he could trust with his life was keeping watch over him. It was embarrassing and comforting at the same time. He knew he was getting overly attached to Quinten and Dare.

But he didn't want to stop it.

Well, part of him did. The part that was sure this wouldn't last. There was no way Quinten would keep him around after Caden was all healed up.

And yet, he couldn't bring himself to care all that much. All he wanted was to wrap himself in the scent of orange blossoms and never leave. It probably should have made him run. It definitely should have made him choose to stay with the Kincaids, at least until he was healed fully. But just the idea had his stomach turning.

Maybe it was because Quinten had been there when he'd been rescued. Or because he'd taken him into his home. Or that he'd brought him to a pack that didn't like or respect him to save Caden's life.

Maybe he'd just imprinted onto his human like a baby duckling, and the intense feelings inside him would fade as he grew stronger.

One thing Kai had said the night before had been true. How could he ever be satisfied living outside of a pack? He didn't know how Dare did it. Wolves were even more social than cats were, but even he and his jaguar needed it. Needed the bonds of pack mates to be strong and healthy, to feel safe and secure.

So it wasn't like he could stay with Quinten long-term. If he tried to, his jaguar would grow weak, and Caden would become resentful, wishing he could get things from Quinten that were impossible. That wouldn't be fair to either of them.

He promised himself that as soon as he was able to, as soon as his instincts weren't latching on to the first safe thing they'd seen, he'd walk away and spare them both the inevitable bad feelings.

And hopefully, his own heartbreak.

He found folded clothes on the end of his bed, another pair of sweats and a plain gray T-shirt. Picking them up, he scurried out of the room and into the bathroom, taking the longest, hottest shower of his life.

As he pulled on the new clothes and sniffed at them, he frowned. They didn't have a hint of orange blossom. At least they didn't smell like anyone else, just laundry detergent, but not the kind they used in the Kincaid house. He was familiar with that scent after sleeping on their sheets last night.

When he stepped out of the steamy bathroom, he found Dare leaning against the wall across the hallway, a cup of coffee in his hand.

Caden looked at him in surprise. "When you weren't outside my bedroom, I thought maybe you were getting some rest before we left."

Dare shook his head and lifted the mug. "Just needed some fuel."

Caden raised both of his eyebrows. "I don't think coffee counts as fuel. Did you eat anything?"

"Would've taken too long."

At that, Caden had to roll his eyes, leading the way down the hallway toward the staircase he'd passed the day before when he'd gone to find Quinten. He could smell bacon and fresh bread permeating the whole house, and it was making his mouth water.

"Well, I'm starving. If you're stuck to me, that means you're going to have to go to the kitchen with me, and you can either eat too, or you can just watch me." He glanced over his shoulder, and he was pretty sure that behind the mug, Dare was grinning at him.

When he lowered it, there was no sign of it.

Caden was pretty sure there had been though. He could tell by the way Dare's eyes had crinkled. He could continue to pretend to be all stoic and unfeeling, but Caden would wear him down.

At the top of the stairs, he slowed. The entrance hall at the bottom was busier than it had been the day before, the whole house humming with activity, even though it was barely 7:30 in the morning.

All the people made him hesitate. He didn't use to mind other people, was great at meeting new ones too—it came with the territory of traveling from pack to pack. He was often the new guy wherever he went, but now the large group of people made him wary.

He wasn't sure he could force himself to go down into that chaos.

"This way," Dare said softly.

Caden turned away gratefully and followed him. After a few twists and turns down some other hallways, they found a much quieter and far less grand set of stairs.

At the bottom, the scent of bacon was almost strong enough that he could taste it in his mouth. He knew they had to be close to the kitchen.

"Do you think it's okay if we just go in and get something?" he asked Dare quietly, not exactly sure why he was whispering.

Dare nodded. "It's fine, kid."

He wrinkled his nose at being called a kid but straightened his shoulders and decided to fake it until he made it.

The kitchen was busy, too, but with far fewer people than the other side of the house had.

There was an older, round woman standing off to the side, giving orders to two younger women. She sent one to refill something in the dining room and the other to wake up "the pups."

Caden hesitated once more just inside. Should they go to the dining room too? It was probably full of Kincaid's people, and he didn't really want to have to make small talk with them or lie once more about not remembering what happened to him.

Before he could decide, Dare nudged him with his arm and then used his chin to point out a small table against the wall. It was set up like a booth at a restaurant, and no one else was sitting there at the moment.

The older woman noticed them, her face creasing in a beaming smile. "Well, good morning," she called, bustling over toward them and wiping her hands on the apron she was wearing. She cast a critical eye over Caden. "You must be starving, dear. Anything in particular you'd like?"

He shook his head, feeling shy in the face of her boisterous good mood. "Whatever you have is fine."

She hummed and looked at Dare. "What about you, wolf?"

He glanced past her into the kitchen and then met her eyes once more. "Bacon."

She laughed and turned away. "Bacon, I can do."

He and Dare settled into either side of the booth, Dare's back to the rest of the kitchen and eyes on the door they'd come through. Caden, on the other hand, got a front-row view of the graceful way the woman ran the entire room.

It seemed like she was doing a million things at once, all while directing the other two. In far less time than he would've thought, she had whipped up a mountain of pancakes and brought it over to the table, then brought another plate full of bacon and then a huge bowl of freshly cut fruit.

He stared, mouth already watering.

Setting empty plates in front of each of them, she nodded. "Go ahead and dig in, dears." She looked at Caden. "You want some coffee or juice, sweetie?"

"Coffee would be great," he said. "Thank you. This looks wonderful."

She smiled at him again, hustling off and coming back with a mug, filling it for him, and topping off Dare's before he could even ask. As soon as she was done, she left again, not lingering over them and making Caden feel self-conscious. Dare was already piling food on his plate, his scarred eyebrow going up when Caden hesitated.

"You heard her. Dig in."

Deciding he wouldn't worry about anything else at the

moment, he did just that, putting four pancakes on his plate, smothering them in syrup, and half a dozen pieces of bacon. He finished that and then gave himself a huge serving of the fruit.

He'd only just started eating that when the door opened behind him, and Dare straightened on his side of the booth. Even without the scent of orange blossoms wafting into his nose, he would've been able to tell it was Quinten.

He could feel his presence, an awareness in the back of his mind, his body warming before he even noticed. He looked up just as Quinten got to the end of the table. He had a suit jacket over his arm and his shirtsleeves rolled up, showing a few of the rune tattoos. His short beard and salt-and-pepper hair were impeccably groomed, and the first couple of buttons on his white shirt were undone, exposing the base of his throat and some of that chest hair he'd so admired the other night.

Caden wasn't staring though.

"When you're finished, we'll take off," he said, checking the time on a watch that had probably been more expensive than Caden's last car. "Arnold is ready whenever."

Caden started to slide out of the booth, ready to get going, but Quinten's hand on his shoulder stopped him. A small smile graced his full lips. "Finish your breakfast, Caden. Then we'll leave."

He debated saying he was done, but the scent of freshly cut pineapple was teasing at his nose. Slowly, he nodded and settled back down. "Okay. I won't be long."

Dare had eaten most of the bacon and a couple of pancakes and picked out a few strawberries from the bowl. He slid out from his side of the booth, wiping delicately at his mouth. "I'll check on Arnold."

Caden watched him leave, a little surprised, but

Quinten was unfazed, leaning a hip against the other side of the booth and pulling his phone out to check something.

Shrugging it off, he quickly finished, hoping they could slip out without anyone noticing and be on their way back to Illinois before he knew it.

———

STEPS FROM FREEDOM, Rick came out of nowhere and raised a hand, silently telling them to stop.

His frustration was probably leaking across the entire entrance hall, but he paused, keeping Quinten just in front of him out of deference.

"Tashmica's in the blue room," Rick said, barely casting Caden a glance. "She examined the note left for you."

Quinten glanced back at him, frowning. "Caden, go find Dare."

He would have rather gone with Quinten, but he didn't argue, not wanting to undermine him in front of the others. Quinten lightly touched his hip, then strode off, spine straight and shoulders back, and Caden couldn't help but watch until he disappeared from view.

Sighing, he only took two steps forward before a voice called, "Wait a second."

He turned, frowning at the stranger. He was human, white, with long blond hair pulled up in a bun on top of his head and an easy smile that immediately put Caden on edge.

"Yes?"

"Caden, right? I just wanted to talk to you for a sec."

He hesitated. Quinten had told him to go find Dare, but he didn't want to be rude and offend Alpha Kincaid. "What about?"

Once he was only a few feet away, the human stopped

and pulled a small cloth bag from his pocket. Caden frowned at it and inhaled, sneezing at the strong scent of herbs and magic. That was a hex bag. Something witches used to make spells transportable or usable by non-magic users.

The man muttered a word, and there was a soft *pop*.

Caden's instincts went crazy. He took several steps back, bringing his hands up to defend himself, but he couldn't get his claws to extend in his weakened state. "Stay back," he hissed.

"Easy, man. I just wanted privacy for this conversation." The blond held up the hex bag. "This prevents anyone outside our little bubble from hearing what we're saying."

"Break it," he snarled, taking another step back, stopping only when his back hit the door.

"In a second. Listen, my name's Gabriel, and I've known Quinten a long time."

"Okay..." That gave Caden pause since it wasn't what he'd been expecting.

Gabriel put his hands in his pockets, doing his best to look as nonthreatening as possible, but there was a deadly aura surrounding him that prevented it. "You don't know him, so I thought I should tell you some things."

Caden pulled his lips back, showing his teeth. "I know him well enough."

He did not appreciate the way Gabriel rolled his eyes at him. "No, you don't. He's not just some weak, innocent human. Quinten Amato is a ruthless businessman who does anything necessary to win."

"And?"

"And," Gabriel dragged the word out, "there are a lot of fucking rumors floating around out there about him, kid. Some really bad shit."

Rumors? Hadn't he said he'd known Quinten for a long time?

"Like what?" he asked, pretending to be interested to see if Gabriel would say anything Caden could use against him.

"All kinds of stuff. There's a reason they call him a mob boss." Gabriel shrugged. "The most persistent are the ones about him being a trafficker."

"Trafficker?"

"Yeah. You know, moving drugs or weapons or even humans illegally or against their will."

Caden's heart sped up. That was a horrible thing to say about someone without an ounce of proof. "You've seen him doing that?"

Looking frustrated, Gabriel sighed. "No, he's more careful than that. Back when I was hunting, if I needed something... ethically questionable, Quinten was the one I called."

Caden stared at him. Did he not understand that spoke more about his own character than Quinten's? "Like what?"

"It doesn't matter—"

"Doesn't it? You're trying to convince me what a terrible person he is, but all you have are rumors and half-truths. Either say something real or break the fucking spell."

Jaw tight, Gabriel stepped closer. "I've seen him hurt people. Torture them for information. Kill them sometimes."

Caden thought about the man from the other night, kneeling on the floor and stinking with fear. He remembered the way Dare had sliced through his throat like it was nothing. How Quinten had told him he'd done well.

How his crime had been hurting someone Quinten cared about.

"Got it," Caden said softly, reaching behind him to grab

the door handle. "This has been fun. Let's not ever do it again, okay?"

He didn't wait for a reply, just ran out of the house as fast as his weak legs would carry him until he heard another *pop*, letting him know the spell had finally broken.

Taking a deep breath, he followed Dare's scent, wanting nothing more than to leave and never see any of the Kincaid Pack again.

Chapter Eight

To get back to Quinten's place, he had to fly in a helicopter for the first time in his life.

He fucking hated it.

As soon as they were in the air, he started to tremble, and he thought he might vomit, even though the pilot was holding the thing steady. The entire flight, his stomach was in his throat, and if he uncovered his eyes to look out even for a second, he'd get lightheaded, his whole body tingling.

Cats were not made to be in the air.

He couldn't imagine how Quinten traveled like this with other shifters, but Dare seemed completely fine. The jerk. He sat opposite him and Quinten, his face impassive as he watched the rushing scenery down below.

Quinten was on his phone most of the time, not looking up, even when Caden buried his face behind his shoulders to block out as much of the experience as he possibly could, burying himself in Quinten's scent and warmth. All he got was a pat on his knee.

When the helicopter finally touched back down on the ground, he pulled his face out of hiding and looked around. They were nowhere near a city.

The helicopter sat in a clearing surrounded by woods. It looked like they were in the middle of the wilderness, but there was a black SUV waiting for them.

"Where are we?" he asked over the sound of the spinning blades as they all disembarked, the pilot, Arnold, not moving.

"We're staying outside the city while you recover," Quinten said, eyes still on his phone.

Caden tried not to feel frustrated. He knew that Quinten was an important man, with a pack and business that needed his attention, but Caden wanted it too, wanted his human to look at him. To see him.

To touch him.

He held back a grumble and followed him and Dare to the SUV. He supposed he should be grateful Quinten and Dare were staying, too, and not just dropping him off and then heading into the city without him. That would have sucked.

As soon as they were well out of the way, the helicopter took off again. They were almost to the vehicle when the driver stepped out.

Caden's head snapped up.

That was no shifter. He paused, inhaling deeply. The other two kept walking toward the man, and as soon as Caden placed the scent, he darted forward, terrified. He planted himself firmly between Quinten and the fucking vampire standing there grinning at them.

He bared his teeth and snarled, crouching defensively. He'd never met a vampire before, though he had heard in his travels that there were a handful left over in Europe after the hunters had done their best to eradicate them all.

The stories about them had survived though, being passed down through packs. Vampires couldn't be trusted, it was said. They could go into bloodlust completely unprovoked and drain and kill anyone near them.

Even though he'd never seen one before, that had to be what the man was. He radiated power in a way that was different than shifters, and there was an earthy scent to him that raised Caden's hackles, an ingrained instinct that hadn't died out.

He was dangerous, that was for sure, but he was also movie-star good-looking with a chiseled jaw, bright blue eyes, and dark hair that was swept back from his face in a way that looked effortless but probably took him an hour.

He eyed Caden like he was an amusing bug that he was considering stomping on. "Well, hello there."

He crossed his arms over his chest, covering the faded words on his T-shirt. Caden didn't think the fact that he was wearing a shirt that said *Bite me* was all that clever or amusing, but maybe vampires were psychopaths by nature.

"Caden." Quinten put a hand on his shoulder and gave it a squeeze.

Caden relaxed despite his better judgment. It was hard for him and his jaguar to stay on edge when Quinten was touching them like that though.

"I'd like you to meet Nero."

Caden glanced back at Quinten and then toward the vampire. "He's with you?" he asked carefully.

"He's with me." There was an edge of humor in Quinten's voice, though his scent stayed fairly mild.

"I've never met one of your kind before." Caden straightened out of his aggressive stance.

Nero's face flickered, his scent becoming overwhelming with pain and sadness. "There aren't many of us left to meet." A moment later, his boyish smile returned, and he glanced at Quinten. "We all set?"

Quinten nodded, and they all loaded into the SUV.

Caden was sitting in the back with Quinten, but he was once again glued to his phone, thumbs typing quickly. Nero and Dare sat in the front, Nero chattering at the silent wolf as they went bumping out of the forest onto a dirt road.

"I can't believe you went into the belly of the beast without me," Nero said sulkily, glancing around the inside of the car.

Dare just grunted, and Quinten smirked a little.

So Caden asked, "What does that mean?"

Nero met his eyes in the rearview mirror. "You went into Kincaid Pack territory. Not just that, but into his home, *and* you lived to tell about it."

Caden glanced sharply at Quinten. "Were we in danger?"

He knew he had been unconscious when they got there and that people had been rude, trying to convince him to stay and talking badly about Quinten, but he hadn't gotten the impression they were in real danger.

Quinten tilted one of his hands back and forth. "You weren't. Dare and I might have been."

"Might have been?" Nero repeated with a snort. "I'm pretty sure Kincaid would've taken the opportunity to wipe you off the map if there weren't so many damn witnesses around."

Quinten shrugged and went back to his phone. Caden looked at him for a while. Why had Quinten risked going there if it was so dangerous? He didn't even know Caden.

Despite the fact the man was still barely paying him any attention, warmth bloomed in his belly. Quinten had risked his life to save *Caden*.

All of the people at the house who'd made snide comments about Quinten, suggested that Caden should stay, or flat out called Quinten a horrible person had been wrong.

Caden couldn't care less what Quinten did in the name of his business. Quinten showed his strength of character when he protected a camboy being abused by his boyfriend and took a strange shifter into his home without hesitation. He showed it when he flew Caden into enemy territory to get him the help he needed to stay alive and never once mentioned how dangerous it was for him.

Goddess, how could so many people be so wrong about him?

"What pack are you from?" Nero asked out of the blue, startling the crap out of him.

A little while ago, they'd turned onto a much busier, paved street, and he'd been captivated by the big, sprawling houses set back from the road.

"Um..." He wasn't sure how much he should share with the vampire. "I don't really have a pack. I'm pretty much a nomad."

Nero's eyes met his again in the rearview, and there was something in his that caught Caden's attention. "Nomad, huh? I've met a few of you in my years."

"Yeah. Well, sometimes it's just easier to keep moving," Caden said, glancing out the window next to him and trying not to remember why he'd needed to leave the pack he'd grown up in.

He could feel the attention of both of the parahumans, so he didn't have to guess that he was giving off some pretty strong scents, but he ignored them, not in the mood to talk.

He felt a hundred times better than he had before they'd gotten the collar off, but after their terrifying flight and the shock at coming face-to-face with a vampire for the first time, he was exhausted. As soon as they got to wherever they were going, he was going to find a bed or a sunny spot and take a nice, long nap.

It wasn't long before Nero was steering the SUV down

a driveway, getting waved through by the man at the huge iron gate. The house that came into view once they passed through was the biggest Caden had ever seen in real life.

The Kincaids' home had been large—three stories and full of people and life—but this was a sprawling estate with outbuildings and more rooms inside than Quinten was probably aware of.

"This is your house?" Caden asked, staring out the window.

"One of them, yes."

One of them, Caden mouthed in awe. He'd known Quinten was wealthy by the way he dressed and how big his apartment had been, but this... this was next-level rich. Who even needed this much house, let alone more than one?

Quinten tucked his phone away and waited for Dare to open his door before stepping out. Instead of going out his own side, Caden scooted across the seat and followed after him, sticking close to his side as they walked up the steps to the large double-doored entrance.

One side opened before they reached it. A severe-looking woman with a short haircut and what was obviously a uniform of a knee-length black skirt, white blouse, and black tie stood in the opening, giving Quinten a brisk nod.

"Mr. Amato," she said. "It's so good to have you home."

"It's always good to be home, Mrs. Burns." He pointed at Caden. "We'll have a guest for a while. This is Caden. Please make sure he's comfortable in one of the bedrooms and that he has anything he needs."

She gave Caden a quick once-over, her expression less than impressed, but she didn't say anything about how he obviously didn't belong in a mansion like this. "Of course, sir. I'll take excellent care of him."

"I know you will," Quinten said, smiling at her as he moved into the house.

The foyer was enormous, three times the size of Rick's, with a grand double staircase curving along the edges and going up to the second floor. Caden stared at what he was pretty sure was a famous painting, just hanging in the entrance of Quinten's house like it was no big deal. How could someone get used to living in a place this huge and imposing?

There were a few scents lingering in the air, but he had a feeling they were all from people that Quinten hired to take care of the place, like Mrs. Burns. It didn't have much of a lived-in feeling, though you'd have to have a family of fifty to achieve that.

It seemed extravagant after some of the places he had lived, but it was beautiful too. Bright and airy. And peaceful. Somehow, he just knew that if given the chance, he could make the sacrifice to get used to the splendor around him.

Except that wouldn't happen. This wasn't and never would be his home. He needed to remind himself it was temporary, and while he appreciated everything Quinten was doing for him, he couldn't forget that.

It didn't stop him from following Quinten like a love-struck puppy.

When Quinten noticed him, he paused and turned around, gesturing back at where Mrs. Burns was still standing. "Go with her, Caden. She'll show you where you'll be staying. You can also give her a list of anything you need, like clothes and a phone, and she'll make sure that you get it."

"But..."

"No buts, kitten. You need to rest. Witch's and doctor's orders."

Caden huffed but relented. He really was tired.

"Follow me," Mrs. Burns said once he'd rejoined her, heading up the left-hand staircase. Her black shoes lightly tapped on each wooden step.

Caden glanced back, but Quinten was already gone. He could just barely hear him say something about a lost container at a port before a door shut and he couldn't hear him at all.

His brows furrowed as he reached the top of the stairs. He would have to do some investigating. He hadn't scented anything when they first came in but for a single door to completely block the noise behind it, there had to be magic involved. How many rooms did Quinten have that were soundproofed?

He supposed it would be convenient to have an office where he could go for privacy, but did he have other rooms like that? Caden wasn't sure he'd like not being able to find him as quickly and easily as he'd want if something was happening.

He could still scent him though. It wasn't like he was completely hidden. Besides, Quinten had a wolf who rarely left his side; it wasn't like he needed Caden to protect him.

Mrs. Burns led him down a couple of hallways, and he knew if he had been human, he would've been lost when he tried to find his way back.

Stopping, she opened a door and gestured him inside. The bedroom was quite large, the bed even bigger than the one he had slept in at Kincaid's house, with a large TV mounted on the wall across from it. Two huge windows looking out into a backyard that had a pool and what looked like a hedge maze were on one wall. There was also an attached bathroom and a walk-in closet.

Altogether, it was bigger than his last apartment.

He inhaled subtly, expecting to find Quinten's scent

embedded in the room. This had to be the main bedroom, didn't it? It was enormous. But all he found was the scent of freshly washed sheets and a little bit of dust.

"If you'd like to rest now, I can come back in a while for your list of necessities," Mrs. Burns said, still in the doorway. "If you need anything before then, you can find me in the kitchen usually."

He nodded, still glancing around at the luxurious room.

She started to back out, pulling the door with her. "After you've had some time to recover, make sure you make your list."

"Oh, I don't need anything," Caden said quickly.

She glanced down at his borrowed sweats. "I think you could use a few things."

Her face didn't change, but there was a hint of humor in her voice and scent.

He wondered if she was making fun of him or if she was just stoic like Dare. "Yeah, I guess," he admitted. "But I don't need a phone or anything. Quinten doesn't have to pay for that stuff for me."

She cocked her head but didn't argue, simply stepped back out into the hall and told him to get some rest. As soon as the door was closed behind her, Caden pulled off his borrowed clothes and walked heavily over to the bed. He peeled back the covers and climbed in, expecting to fall right to sleep.

That was not the case.

He tossed and turned for probably an hour before he finally gave up and dragged himself back out of bed, somehow even more tired than he had been before. He pulled his sweatpants back on but didn't bother with his shirt and headed out.

It took him a while, but he was able to use his nose to find a room that had a lingering scent of orange blossoms seeping from it. He carefully pushed open the door and peered inside, not expecting to find Quinten but not wanting to bother him if he was in there.

Okay, yeah, this was obviously the master bedroom.

It was easily twice as wide as the room Caden had been given, with a bed just as big and a sitting area next to a wall that was made up of glass.

He inhaled deeply, and his eyes fell to half-mast. By the time he pulled his sweats back off and climbed under the covers, he was already falling asleep.

Chapter Nine

Quinten rubbed at his throbbing temples and ignored the way Dare and Nero were still half-heartedly sniping at each other. The two of them had the strangest friendship. For the most part, they got along just fine. But every once in a while, Nero seemed to get some sort of sick pleasure at poking at the wolf, trying to get him riled up.

Even less often, Dare let him.

Luckily, they weren't going at it too hard, Nero just teasing Dare about their trip to Kincaid's territory.

Quinten had just gotten off the phone with the fifth person he'd had to call since he'd arrived at his house, but the shipping container issue was finally resolved. He usually wouldn't have had to personally deal with something like that, but the container in question held materials for his... less-than-legal side of the business. He'd been worried it had been accidentally loaded onto another ship, but they finally found it in the wrong spot at the shipping yard. Soon, all of the cargo would be unloaded and sent off to where it needed to be, making him a shit ton of money.

"What time is it?" he asked without opening his eyes.

"About 6:30," Nero said. "Why?"

Quinten sighed. "Robbie will be home soon."

Neither one said anything at that, and he finally glanced up and saw they were exchanging looks.

"Robbie's here?" Dare asked. "I thought he was in Mexico still."

Quinten shook his head. After graduating from college last month, Robbie had been gone on trips with friends more than he'd been home. "He got back late last week."

Neither said anything, exchanging another look he couldn't read.

"Is that going to be a fucking problem?" he snapped, his patience having left him three phone calls ago.

"No, sir," Nero said, shaking off the strange look on his face.

Dare shook his head, but his jaw was tight, and Nero's fingers were tapping on the arms of his chair. He didn't know what was up with the two of them, but he didn't have the energy to get into it.

He pushed to his feet and started for the door. "Mrs. Burns should have dinner ready shortly, if either of you are hungry."

He knew Dare would eat with them, but Nero could be weird about consuming food in front of other people. People had the misconception, based on human myths, that vampires only drank blood, but real vampires could supplement their diets with certain other foods. They couldn't tolerate everything that humans and shifters could eat, but for the most part, they could share a meal if they wanted to, but he knew that it made Nero uncomfortable to have people staring at him when he did, and Caden seemed wary enough of him to do just that.

"I'll pass," Nero said, unsurprisingly. "I'll head out and grab myself a bite."

100

Quinten raised a brow, glancing down at his shirt. He shook his head when Nero just laughed, leaving the room so fast he turned into nothing but a blur.

Vampires could be weird, that was for sure.

He didn't blame them though. After being nearly driven to extinction and having to go into hiding for decades, it made sense it would take a chunk out of their collective psyche.

Dare silently followed him out of his office.

Should he go and check on Caden before they sat down for dinner? He'd assumed the jaguar would have made an appearance hours ago, but they hadn't seen him since they'd arrived. He didn't want to bother him if he was still sleeping. Before he'd left Kincaid's, Tashmica had reminded him not to let him do anything strenuous for days, no shifting for a week.

Quinten hadn't said anything, but he did wonder what qualified as *strenuous* to a shifter according to a witch, but he figured he would just make Caden stay in bed and feed him plenty of food until he'd regained his strength. Which he would, despite what some alpha-mates thought.

He was almost to the dining room when he heard a loud gasp and then running feet. "Oh my god, why didn't you tell me you were coming?"

He turned just before a tiny, lean body ran into him, arms coming around to squeeze him tightly.

Chuckling, Quinten hugged him back. "We just got here a few hours ago. I thought it would be a nice surprise for you."

Robbie huffed, pretending indignation, but he squeezed Quinten even tighter. "I'm so glad to see you. I keep meaning to get into the city and stay at the penthouse for a couple of days, but either you're off doing business somewhere, or I was with my friends."

101

He sounded a little guilty, but Quinten didn't want that. He rubbed a hand over the back of Robbie's head. "Don't worry about it. Now that you're done with school, we'll be able to see each other more if you want."

"Duh," Robbie said, then laughed and pushed away just enough that he could peer up at Quinten. "What brought on this surprise visit?"

A low growl came from behind him. It was primal and terrifying, Quinten's instincts prickling the hair on the back of his neck. He whipped around, keeping Robbie behind him, and was shocked to find Caden in the doorway, eyes glowing and fangs bared.

Despite the aggression, Quinten's body heated at the familiar gym shorts sitting low on Caden's hips, the rest of his pale skin on full display.

He had half a mind to tell Dare to avert his eyes, which was ridiculous. They'd all seen him fully naked at the warehouse, and shifters weren't bothered about nakedness like humans were.

It bothered Quinten though. He couldn't help the possessiveness gnawing at his gut any more than he could have stopped himself from protecting Robbie.

"Caden—"

Glowing golden eyes turned on him, drawing him up short. "Who the fuck is that?"

Oh shit. He knew what was happening. Pressing his lips together, he did his best to shut down the thrill sparking in his chest at the fact that Caden had been jealous.

Maybe he was as terrible as everyone said.

He stepped away from Robbie, knowing Dare had him covered. Caden wasn't really a threat though. Not really, and definitely not after he understood what he'd walked in on.

Pointing to the ground in front of him, he said calmly, "Come here, kitten."

Caden looked behind him at Robbie and then back at Quinten before darting forward. He stopped right in front of him, barely any space left between them. Slowly, Quinten settled his palm against the side of Caden's neck.

Immediately, his eyes dimmed, and his canines shrank back to their regular size. His body wavered for a second, like a cattail in the breeze, and then he was pressing his face into Quinten's throat and inhaling deeply. His exhale was shuddery, a tiny sound pressing into his thin skin. Needy fingers grabbed at his suit jacket, wrinkling it all to shit, no doubt, but he couldn't care less.

"How are you feeling?" he asked, keeping his hold on the side of Caden's neck and wrapping his other arm around his waist. The bare skin of his hip was so warm he almost jerked his hand away in shock.

"Fine," Caden grumbled as he nuzzled closer.

"That's good," he said. "There's someone I want you to meet."

Caden stiffened against him.

Quinten gave his neck a squeeze in reassurance and then slowly separated their bodies. When he turned, he found Dare planted between them and Robbie. His eyes locked on Caden.

"Stand down, Dare," Quinten said firmly.

"Yeah," Robbie added, slapping at his arm and stepping up next to him. He rolled his eyes. "Always so overprotective."

Quinten didn't miss the fact that Robbie didn't actually look all that annoyed and suppressed a sigh. He was pretty sure he'd had a crush on Dare for years, and he just knew one day it was going to break Robbie's heart.

"Caden," Quinten said. "This is Robert."

"I go by Robbie," he interjected quickly, sending Quinten a glare.

"He does." Quinten smiled at him and then turned to his prickly cat. "Robbie, this is Caden."

"It's nice to meet you," Caden said stiffly.

"Wow, not even I believe that, and I just have dull human senses."

Quinten suppressed a laugh. "Caden, Robbie is my son."

Caden's head jerked around to stare at him wide-eyed, and then he looked back at Robbie. They didn't look much alike, he'd give him that.

His son had gotten his height and build from his mother and barely topped out at five foot three compared to Quinten's six two. His hair naturally had loose curls, and he kept it cut short on the sides, spending a lot of Quinten's money on different hair products to keep the longer section on top just the way he liked it.

His skin had just the barest hint of a tan year-round, a throwback to his mother's Mediterranean heritage from a few generations back, but it was his eyes that always caught people's attention. Just like his mother, he had the most gorgeous violet eyes. Most people assumed they were contacts. Sometimes, parahumans thought they were from a spell and tried to get him to share his secret.

His round cheeks made him look younger than his twenty-two years, especially since—much to his dismay—he couldn't grow facial hair to save his life.

Quinten had never loved anyone the way he loved his son, not even Liam, who he would die or kill for.

He'd only been a sixteen-year-old idiot when he knocked up his girlfriend. A few months after she gave birth to Robert, she'd disappeared. He wasn't sure what exactly had happened to her, if she just couldn't handle being a teenage mom, if her family had moved her away so she could start over somewhere. No one ever told him, and he hadn't bothered looking for her once he had the means. She'd left them and never looked back.

Thankfully, his parents and Callie had helped him so that he could finish high school and then college, making sure Robbie had everything he needed growing up.

Most people outside his inner circle had no idea that he had a kid, let alone one that he'd had when he was a teenager. He'd been careful to keep Robbie safe as he'd started expanding his business into the grayer area of importing. It had been important to him to make sure that Robbie could have any future he wanted, even if he wanted nothing to do with the family business.

Caden kept staring, having a hard time processing, it seemed, and then his face flushed bright pink, and his eyes dropped to the ground. "I'm so sorry for growling at you."

Robbie laughed. "Hey, it's not the first time, and it definitely won't be the last. Have you met this guy?" His son pointed his thumb over his shoulder at Dare. "Every time I see him, I swear he growls at me, just so grumpy," Robbie teased and then clapped his hands together. "Okay, I'm starving, and I want to hear all about how this happened." He waved a hand between Caden and Quinten.

Quinten frowned. "There's no—"

"Yeah, yeah, yeah," Robbie said, flying past him. "Save it for dinner. Mrs. Burns!"

He disappeared, presumably to harangue Quinten's housekeeper into feeding him immediately.

"We're all screwed," Dare muttered as he passed him.

Caden still looked shocked, like he had a million questions, but Quinten just sighed and gestured for him to go ahead of him. "There's no point in keeping the boy waiting. He always gets what he wants."

"Um, yeah. Okay."

By the time dinner ended, Robbie and Caden appeared to be best friends. They were chatting nonstop about shows, books, and famous people on the internet that Quinten had never heard of.

He also realized that Caden was only a year older than his son, which made him feel gross until he reminded himself there was nothing between him and Caden. The jaguar turning to him for comfort was natural after what had happened. It didn't mean anything more. The jealousy from before... He was sure that was just some misguided instincts.

Besides, a lot of the shifters in his life drew comfort from his touch. He might not be an alpha, but he was still an authority figure for their tight-knit group. They were all bonded in a way, even if it wasn't quite like a pack.

After dinner, the two younger men had darted off together. It hadn't taken Quinten long to find them though.

He was leaned against the doorway of his library, watching Robbie race around and pull out all of his favorite books, shoving them at Caden every time he passed him until Caden was holding a stack at least ten deep. Robbie was still going, cracking jokes and pulling Caden into his web. His son was a hundred times more personable than him, always smiling and laughing and making friends wherever he went.

He was glad they got along. It soothed something inside him that he hadn't realized had been anxious. He was about to step in and join them, maybe give Caden a couple of his own favorites, when Dare stepped up next to him.

"Dominic's on the phone."

Quinten nodded and took a step back, giving one last look at the pair and meeting Caden's eyes for a second before the jaguar smiled at him and turned back to Robbie.

As he made his way to his office, Quinten tried to decide what was in that smile. Maybe affection? No, it had been more than that. Caden had looked... happy but in a deeper way. Almost satisfied. That seemed strange. Why would he be satisfied by having dinner and getting books from Quinten's son? As he entered his office, he shoved the silly thoughts away.

He took Dare's phone from him, put it on speaker, and then set it on the desk between them. "What have you found out, Dom?"

The wolf sighed over the line. "Well, I know who he is, sort of."

"What does that mean?" Quinten asked, exchanging a frustrated look with Dare.

"It means that Ash had to use some of his contacts, but we finally found him."

"Okay, and who is he?"

"He's just some soldier in the Borko family."

"A soldier?" Quinten asked, brows furrowed.

He'd known it had to have been someone either not affiliated with the crime family or someone so low in the organization he'd never heard of them, but that still didn't explain why someone with real responsibility in the organization would target him.

Or why they'd use Caden to do it.

It didn't make any sense.

"What else have you found?"

"Well, word is he's Miloš's bastard from some mistress he had thirty years ago."

"He's Miloš's son?" Dare asked, leaning closer to the phone.

"Apparently, and there's also some whispers that he might be the one who killed the old man." Dominic chuckled. "Well, people not saying you did it are saying he might have."

Quinten rolled his eyes. "We already know I didn't do it."

"Yeah, but a lot of people think you did," Dom said. "But others are quietly saying that it was this Tiho because he's been doing shit to move up in the family ever since."

"Why hadn't he climbed before his dad died?" Quinten mused out loud. "Even bastards of bosses are given cushy, high-ranking positions."

"No one could really say," Dominic said. "At least not any of Ashe's sources. There was one woman who said she met him one time and she would swear on a stack of bibles that he was a straight-up psychopath."

Quinten frowned. "You would think that would mean Miloš would move him up faster, use him as a weapon."

"The impression I got," Dom said carefully, "was that there was concern he couldn't be controlled, that his impulses were stronger than his obedience."

Quinten nodded, rolling that information over in his head. "It still doesn't make sense to me," he finally said out loud. "Why kill his father and then come after me in such a strange way?"

Dare shrugged, and Dominic said over the line, "I don't know. Nobody's heard anything about what happened or the little gift he left you at the warehouse. Whatever he's doing to you, he's not sharing it, not even within the family."

Quinten hummed and then asked, "Did you get contact information for him?"

"I got a previously known address, but Ash and I checked it out, and it was abandoned. I've also got a phone number. I'm not sure it's working anymore."

"Give it to me," Quinten said, copying down the numbers as he rattled them off. "I'm not playing whatever

108

games this sick fucker wants to try and draw me into. If he wants to be the new head of the family, then he has to follow the same goddamn rules his father did. If he won't... Well, then, we'll show him who really owns the city, won't we?"

Dare grunted in agreement, always down for a little bloodshed.

Clearing his throat, Dom said, "I get that, man, but maybe we should wait and see if I can find out any more information. Ash says he has a few more sources that he could check with."

Quinten shook his head, even though Dom couldn't see him. "Keep looking, but I'm not waiting. I don't want to give the impression, even for a second, that something like this can go unanswered."

"You're right. Okay, I'll keep looking."

"You've done good work," Quinten told him. "Thank you for using Ash."

Dominic chuckled. "That fucker is crazy, but not so bad... for a necromancer."

Dare spoke up right before Quinten hung up. "See if his mother is still alive and where she is."

There was silence on the other end for a long moment, and then Dom said, "Alright, you got it," and hung up.

Quinten eyed him and then typed the phone number Dom had given him into Dare's phone. "Should I be worried about you bringing his mother into this?"

Dare shrugged but didn't answer.

Quinten let it go, setting the ringing phone back on the desk. He thought it was going to go to voicemail, but it picked up at the last second. "Who the fuck is this, and how'd you get this number?"

The voice on the other line sounded nothing like his father. Miloš had emigrated from Serbia half a century ago but maintained a thick accent his whole life. This guy sounded like every other American Quinten did business with.

Cocky. Aggressive.

"This is Quinten Amato," he said, keeping his voice even and hard. "I got your message, Tiho."

There was nothing but crackling on the other end for a moment, at least nothing that he could hear. Dare had his eyes closed and was leaning over the device with his head turned so his ear was just above it, listening intently for any clues in the background.

"Quinten! I wasn't expecting your call," Tiho said cheerfully.

"I can't imagine why not." Quinten settled into the chair behind his desk. "You left me a nice present after all and a signed note. Did you think I wouldn't be able to find you because you're some low-level street thug barely worth your father's notice?"

There was a sound on the line, almost like a choked-off yell or growl, and then there was nothing.

"It's muted," Dare said lowly. "Somebody's with him. I could hear them breathing in the background."

"Interesting," Quinten said, and then they waited.

Finally, Tiho came back and said hoarsely, "Well, I just figured you would be too busy to come track me down."

"Too busy?" he said, feigning confusion.

"Yeah," Tiho said impatiently. "Dealing with that cat. Is he still alive?"

The confirmation that Tiho had known exactly what Caden was sent a chill down his spine.

"He is."

"He's got to be getting pretty close to death." There was a sneer in Tiho's voice and a coldness that Quinten rarely encountered even in some of the dirtier business he dealt in.

This man truly didn't care that Caden could have been dying an excruciating, slow death right at that moment.

"No, he's just fine," Quinten said, forcing cheer into his voice. "Last I saw him, he was grabbing a book from the library."

There was another long pause, but this time, he could still hear a faint noise, so he knew it wasn't muted. Tiho was just surprised. "Good. That's great. I'm so relieved to hear it," Tiho said, sounding anything but. "You know, I was really worried when I found him like that."

"Found him?" Quinten asked. "Is that what we're going with?"

"What do you mean?"

"I mean," Quinten said, letting an edge of steel into his voice, "that you're the sick fucker who put that collar on him. We both know it. Don't pretend. I don't have time for games. Unlike you, I have actual responsibilities that I have to take care of. So let's cut to the chase, Tiho. What the fuck do you want, and why should I give it to you and not just kill you?"

"You've got it all wrong, man." Tiho started talking faster, scrambling. "I swear, I didn't put that on him."

Dare shook his head, but Quinten didn't need him to confirm that it was a lie.

"Tiho, that's strike two. You need to be honest with me, or this conversation is going to be over."

The line went dead again, and Dare straightened. "Why is he lying?"

"I'm not sure, but I don't appreciate it. It does make me concerned that he has some longer plan at work."

"Or the person with him does."

Quinten conceded that with a quick nod. He waited another few seconds and then hung up before immediately calling back.

Tiho answered, "Sorry, my phone—"

"Shut up." Quinten planted his hands on the desk and rose to his feet. "This was slightly amusing for a moment, but now it's over. You come near me, my people, my ports, my fucking *city*, and I will put an end to you and anyone you've ever talked to, cared about, or worked with."

"Quinten—"

"I don't give a shit what you want, Tiho. I was lying. It doesn't matter because if I ever hear your name again, I will kill you. I'll do it even slower than that fucking collar would have. Hell, maybe I'll have one of my witches whip something up that's similar."

"Listen," Tiho said, "that's not what happened. You see, I was going to this—"

Quinten didn't wait to hear what new bullshit he was going to spew, hanging up.

"That was useless," Dare said, taking his phone back.

"Maybe. Though the fact that he wouldn't admit to what he did was telling. We'll talk to Caden and see what he remembers and go from there." He smiled sharply. "I'm inclined to do the Borko family a favor and wipe this piece of shit off the face of the planet for them."

"They might appreciate that."

Quinten tugged at the cuffs of his jacket and moved around his desk. "If he's making a play for the top, I definitely think Vlatko would. When I send him his half brother in pieces, he might not be as thankful, but it'll get the point across. Fuck with me, and you'll find out what happens."

"The Borkos may go to war with us on principle."

"And then the Borkos will learn that I have been extraordinarily kind to them, allowing them to do business in *my* territory. It was convenient having somebody keep the other families from trying to establish themselves back in

Chicago, and taking a percentage of their dealings added nicely to the coffers, but we don't need them." He stopped in front of Dare and held his eyes. "We. Don't. Need. Them. We can protect our territory without them. If they prove to be more trouble than they're worth, then we will take out every single one of them. It'll send a clear message to everyone—in and outside the city—that this is our territory, and we will hold it. By blood if necessary."

"By blood," Dare repeated, lowering his eyes and tipping his head to expose his neck.

Quinten appreciated the show of submission, but it wasn't necessary. He clapped the side of Dare's neck and gave it a squeeze, then moved past him toward the door. "I want you to call Vlatko Borko and tell him that if he doesn't get his brother in line, there will be consequences."

"He wouldn't take Dom's call," Dare reminded him, opening the office door for him.

"Tell him if I have to take the time to call him personally, he will not like what happens, and then see if he knows anything of use."

Dare nodded.

"And then I want you to get some rest. You didn't sleep at all last night."

"I'm fine," Dare said, pulling his phone back out.

"You're always fine," Quinten said with a smile, "but do as you're told anyway."

Dare rolled his eyes and put his phone to his ear. "Yes, sir."

Quinten smiled and headed for the stairs, intent on doing nothing more for the day except take off his suit and pass the fuck out. He didn't encounter anybody on his way up to his room, the house quiet. He wouldn't be surprised if Caden had gone back to bed after whatever adventures he and Robbie had gotten up to. His son was either camped out in his room playing video games, or he'd gone out for the evening.

He tried not to worry about him, knowing that Robbie was a grown man, but he still checked his phone to see where it said Robbie was. The tension in his shoulders eased when it showed that Robbie's phone was right there at the house with him.

He slipped into his bedroom and didn't bother turning on a light, stripping out of his suit and jumping into the shower to quickly wash off the day.

The hot water barely touched the strain in his muscles, but he was pretty used to that. It had been years since he was able to truly relax. He had too many responsibilities on his shoulders, relaxation becoming a luxury he couldn't afford. He was fine with that though, even on the days when he had to deal with a nuisance like Tiho. He would rather this life than one that was monotonous.

He craved the adrenaline and the power, and he loved the money. And he didn't care that it probably made him a terrible person, but he liked feeling as powerful as—if not more so—than the people he had to contend with. People like the Borkos or the Kincaid Pack who thought they were special or that they deserved things because of their last name or where they'd been born. What they'd been born as.

He called bullshit.

Sure, he hadn't exactly grown up poor, but he'd still clawed his way to the top. In a world that viewed his kind as weak and indispensable, parahumans across the country feared him, and he would never give that up. It offered protection for his son, for his brother, for his tight-knit group of friends.

As he climbed into bed, he became aware of someone else breathing in the room with him just before a warm body rolled into him.

He stiffened as arms wrapped around him, naked flesh pressing to his own.

Soft lips brushed against the thin skin of his throat, a sleep-hoarse voice muttering, "There you are. What took you so long?"

Chapter Ten

"What are you doing here, Caden?"

He grumbled and pressed even closer, burrowing as deeply into Quinten's warmth as he could get, wishing he could disappear under his skin and sleep there for days. "Trying to sleep," he mumbled.

"Caden," Quinten said slowly, "why are you in my bed?"

"Smells better." His sleepy brain felt like that answer was obvious, and he almost tacked on a *duh* but yawned instead.

Quinten didn't respond right away, and he wasn't touching Caden back. His body was stiff as a board, arms at his sides, and his scent was fluctuating like crazy.

Caden lifted his head up and squinted at him through bleary eyes. "What's wrong?"

"You shouldn't be in here," Quinten said firmly, but his face softened as he looked at Caden.

Pain twisted in Caden's chest. "Do you want me to leave?" he asked quietly.

It hoped desperately that he didn't.

He knew that as soon as Quinten wrapped his arms around him, he'd be able to fall into a deep, dreamless sleep. His nap that afternoon hadn't been all that restful, awful memories mixing with fears twisting up and producing nightmares that wouldn't leave him be.

"You have your own bedroom. You don't need to stay in mine."

"I know... but I want to," Caden said, frowning. "Do you want me to leave?"

He repeated the question, studying Quinten's face, but he wasn't giving anything away. Inhaling deeply, he did his best to decipher his scent. Quinten didn't smell angry, just confused and tired with the lightest thread of arousal hidden way down deep.

Was that why he was making such a fuss? Did he think Caden would be upset?

Silly human.

Caden snuggled back down and threw his leg over one of Quinten's, pressing himself as close as he could possibly get into his warm, fragrant skin and sighing happily.

Quinten groaned, his fingers wrapping around one of Caden's biceps and squeezing.

For a second, he thought Quinten was going to push him away, that he'd separate their bodies and demand Caden get out of his bed, out of his room, maybe even out of his house. That he'd overstepped and broken some sacred human rule.

In the shifter world, when you needed comfort, you got it from your pack, those you felt safest with. Even if he didn't have a pack, Quinten made him feel safe, so he'd followed his nose and his instincts and come back to his bed to wait for him.

He didn't shove him away.

Quinten let out a slow breath, and his fingers relaxed.

So slowly Caden thought he was imagining it at first, Quinten's hand slid up until it crested his shoulder before slipping over until he was cupping the back of Caden's neck. Then he squeezed.

Caden whimpered.

He couldn't help it.

He felt like... he didn't even know. It was almost like a cub being held securely by somebody of authority in his pack. He wasn't a cub, but... that's what it reminded him of. The firm hold, maybe a gentle shake for attention. Though there was a possessiveness in Quinten's grip that didn't remind him of being a cub *at all*.

He was just so tired, not just physically but mentally. All of the things that he'd been through for the last few months were weighing him down, exhausting him, making it hard for him to turn the next page. He wanted to hand all of that stuff over to Quinten and let him have it. He was already so good at dealing with all kinds of problems and people. Caden was sure that he would handle a little bit more just fine.

His body relaxed even more the longer Quinten held his nape. He inhaled orange blossoms and exhaled all his worries and fears.

For the night, he was going to imagine that he could do that. That Quinten would let him hand over his problems, and he'd shoulder the responsibility of Caden and the mess of his life. That Caden would be able to breathe again. He could live inside the scent of Quinten's skin, run through the hedge maze in the backyard as his jaguar, hang out with his son, get comfortable enough with Dare to truly tease him.

He let himself imagine those things because he knew when morning came, he would have to let them go and pretend he didn't want them at all.

CADEN COULDN'T MOVE.

He could barely breathe, a weight pressing on his chest, constricting his lungs and forcing his heart to work faster and faster.

Everything hurt, but especially the deep gashes right over his left hip. That cheetah had been fierce and nearly taken Caden down. But he'd somehow managed to survive, and now he was in the Gray Room, the place that was even worse than all the other horrors of the place.

His breathing came faster, and black dots covered his vision. He was hyperventilating. He knew it, but he couldn't stop it. All he could see was the bright gray of the ceiling, his arms fully extended and strapped down. He shivered uncontrollably. The cold metal table he was forced to lie on naked never warmed, no matter how long they kept him here.

Sometimes it felt like days.

He couldn't see anyone, but he could feel that something was there, getting closer.

Oh goddess, please. He just wanted to go home. Why couldn't they just kill him already?

Something wet and freezing landed on his thigh with a soft *plop* and began slithering up his leg. It was a whisper over his skin, leaving behind a cold, aching feeling and stealing the warmth right from his body everywhere it touched.

He craned his head up, trying to see. He had just enough leeway in his restraints to see down the length of his body. A cry of horror ripped from his mouth, his sore throat tearing at the volume and force.

Thick, black sludge was dripping from the ceiling over his legs, where it was collecting and growing bigger, moving rhythmically as it slowly made its way up his body. As he stared at it, the sludge wobbled back and forth, and Caden sucked in a breath.

It was watching him right back.

He screamed and tugged at the restraints holding his limbs down, but there was no give. There was never any give. Goddess, what was that shit?

He'd thought he'd lost his will to fight against the assholes holding him captive, but as the blackness oozed up his body, making his skin burn from frostbite and his bones start to ache, he knew he had a little fight left in him after all.

As the thing crested his pecs, he cried out again, begging for someone to help him but knowing exactly what was going to happen. It would cover his mouth, and his nose, and his eyes, pressing, pressing, pressing until he couldn't breathe or see or speak.

Suffocate him slowly, alone in this room full of remembered pain, in this place where he'd barely survived.

He started to scream, over and over again. His struggles against the bindings were growing weak, all the energy sucked from him at the intense cold. He was going numb, nothing but sharp prickles left.

Oh goddess, it was almost to his mouth.

The mound of ooze arched above him, thinning and spreading until it shadowed his whole head just inches above him. He sucked in harsh breaths—and then froze.

That wasn't black ooze.

No. No, no, no, no, no!

He screamed and strained to move his head away. "I'm sorry! Please, don't! I'm so sorry!"

The thick layer of dark red blood pulsed angrily. The coppery scent was filling his nose. He could already taste it in the back of his throat.

He wouldn't be able to breathe.

He wouldn't be able to breathe.

He couldn't breathe!

"Caden! Wake up."

He jolted awake, a cry on his lips, and scrambled to get out from underneath the blankets. He needed to uncover his whole body. Somehow, he was overheating and freezing at the same time, his body slick with sweat, even as his teeth chattered.

He threw the covers off him and ran his fingers over his legs and his wrists, touching his chest and his throat. He could see in the pre-dawn gray light seeping into the room that there was nothing on him, that it had just been a bad dream.

There was no black sludge or suffocating glob of blood. There never was.

But there had been a Gray Room.

"Caden, look at me."

He jerked his head around and met Quinten's worried eyes.

"Are you alright?"

He nodded, feeling so disjointed and confused he wasn't sure what to say. "Sorry for waking you. I'll go."

He started to crawl out of the bed, but Quinten wrapped an arm around him from behind and pulled him back into the warmth of his embrace. He expected to feel claustrophobic—that's how he usually was when he woke up from one of his nightmares. When he was still at the Bad Place, he'd pace as much as he could, wishing to be able to open a window for a single breath of fresh air.

But instead, feeling the warmth of Quinten's body pressed all down his back, feeling his lungs expanding and his scent filling his nose as one of his big hands rubbed

Caden's abs gently, he relaxed faster than he ever had before.

Sinking back against Quinten's body, he sighed. "Sorry," he mumbled again.

Quinten ran his nose up the back of Caden's ear. "Quit apologizing. Did you have a nightmare?"

He nodded, pulling Quinten's arm over him more fully. He wanted to be smothered by him, which didn't make sense, considering what had been terrifying him in that dream. But that's what he wanted. He wanted to cease to exist as Caden for a while and just sink into Quinten's body. He wanted to be shielded by it, protected.

"Will you tell me about it?"

He shook his head. "I can't," he said wetly, fighting the urge to cry. "Not right now."

"Tomorrow?"

It was in the form of a question, but Caden knew that it was more of a demand. He'd had a feeling that Quinten had known he'd been lying when he'd told the Kincaid and his witches that he didn't remember anything, yet the idea of laying out everything that had happened to him exhausted him even before he started.

A small part of him was also worried about what Quinten—and even Dare—would think about him after they knew. They were both so strong and formidable. What had happened to Caden never would've happened to either of them. They wouldn't have allowed themselves to be taken to that place to be used like an animal.

"Tomorrow," Caden whispered.

Quinten nuzzled into the back of his neck. "Well, later today."

Caden huffed out a soft laugh. "What time is it?"

"Way too early. Go back to sleep."

He rubbed his lips together and stared at the wall ahead of him. "I don't think I can. I'm still a little... wound up."

He was scared, but he couldn't force himself to say that. Quinten had probably never been scared of anything in his life.

"I'm right here," Quinten said softly. "You don't have to be... wound up."

Of course he knew the truth. Caden had probably been whimpering and crying in his sleep, maybe even screaming. He tried not to feel embarrassed, telling himself for the millionth time it wasn't his fault that he'd gotten taken. That he'd only done what he'd needed to so he could survive.

It... almost worked.

Quinten disentangled his hand from Caden's hold just enough that he could move his palm up and press it flat over where Caden's heart was still beating too fast. He took a big, deep, exaggerated breath, his chest expanding against Caden's back, and then let it out slowly. He did it again, and Caden copied him without thinking.

They breathed like that for a while, neither saying anything. It took almost half an hour, but Caden finally was able to settle down. He relaxed into the bed, scooting back until his ass was pressed against Quinten's groin.

"Can you pull the covers back up? I'm cold." He said it quietly, his voice soft in a way it wasn't usually.

Quinten didn't say anything, but he sat up and grabbed the covers from where Caden had tossed them aside and carefully covered them both before realigning their bodies underneath and wrapping his arm back around Caden.

His hold felt good, possessive. Caden let out a tired breath. Maybe he would be able to fall asleep again after all.

"Do you want to tell me the real reason why you're in my bed?" Quinten murmured, just before Caden was going to drift off.

"I told you," he slurred. "It smells better."

"Caden." Quinten sighed, his scent taking on an edge of frustration.

All the happy, gooey feelings Caden had been swimming in on the way to dreamland began to ebb. "I don't know what you want me to say."

"The truth would be nice."

He drew a star on the back of Quinten's hand with one of his fingers as he considered that. His room did smell better; that was the truth, though it was only half of it.

Quietly, he said, "You make me feel safe. I haven't been safe in a long time, but you make me feel that way. Right now... I just need to be near you. That's as much truth as I can give you."

Quinten didn't say anything, not for a long moment. Caden could practically hear the seconds ticking by. Finally, Quinten pressed his lips to the back of Caden's neck and gave him a soft kiss and then another as he moved just a fraction of an inch over.

And then another, and then another.

Caden shivered in his hold as Quinten pressed kiss after kiss into his skin, all the way to the rounded edge of his shoulder, and then he started making his way back.

"Quinten," he moaned, not sure what had happened, what had changed, but not upset about it *at all*.

"I make you feel safe," Quinten said, almost like he couldn't believe it.

"Of course you do," Caden said breathlessly, arching his back to press more firmly against the growing length pressing into him. "You make everyone around you feel safe."

Quinten huffed a laugh as he reached the curve of Caden's throat and gave a soft nip that sent tingles down his spine and out to his fingertips. "I most definitely do not make everyone around me feel safe."

Okay, yeah, that was probably true. There was a reason people called him a mobster, after all.

"The people you care about, the ones you keep close." He didn't dare call them a pack, though the more time he spent around Quinten and those he associated with, the more he could see it. Kai had been wrong, he was pretty sure, but he didn't bring it up. Not when there was a scorching hot man getting aroused in bed with him.

Quinten hummed and then snagged Caden's earlobe between his teeth. "Say it again."

"What?" Caden asked breathlessly, losing the thread of the conversation as his body heated to boiling.

"Say that I make you feel safe again."

Caden was nodding before he even finished asking, reaching back with one of his hands to thread his fingers into that salt-and-pepper hair that drove him crazy in the best possible way.

"You do. Quinten, *you do*. When I'm next to you... I know it doesn't make sense, but I know you'll protect me." He moaned raggedly as Quinten tugged sharply on his ear. "Goddess. I don't think I've ever felt this safe in my life."

Quinten groaned and rolled into him, pressing his front into the soft mattress beneath them and plastering himself to Caden's back. Without thought, Caden spread his legs, making room for Quinten between them.

"A lot of people would call you misguided for feeling that way," Quinten said conversationally, but his voice wasn't as steady as it had been before.

"A lot of people can fuck off and leave us alone."

Quinten laughed. "Agreed."

Caden opened his mouth, on the verge of confessing what Gabriel had said to him before he'd left Rick's house, but thank the goddess, Quinten stopped him by rolling his hips and rubbing himself at the cleft of Caden's ass.

"Is this—"

"Yes. Goddess yes. More, please," Caden begged, doing his best to arch his low back to make Quinten's movements easier, but he was heavy for a human, holding him firmly in place.

Why did he love that so much?

"So eager, kitten."

Another thing he loved that other people would probably think he shouldn't.

Screw them.

When Quinten called him kitten, he felt special and cared for. He didn't care what anyone else thought about it.

He nodded, face half-smooshed in his pillow. He grabbed it and tossed it away to breathe easier, then relaxed back down, letting his body go pliant beneath Quinten's broader one.

The tickle of chest hair against his back made him shiver and squirm.

"I love how soft your skin is," Quinten mumbled before swiping his tongue up Caden's spine.

"Oh shit." He wiggled a little more, desperate for some friction on his dick.

To his utter disappointment, the amazing heat of Quinten's body disappeared. He whimpered and craned his head around, nearly swallowing his tongue at what he saw. Quinten was kneeling between Caden's knees, fist wrapped around his cock tightly, stroking himself.

"I thought..." He couldn't even finish his thought, so transfixed by the thick, veiny length in Quinten's hand. It was long, too, and cut, with just a little wetness at the slit. Goddess...

"Answer me something first, kitten."

"Hmm?" Would Quinten's come taste like orange blossoms too? He licked his lips, imagining taking the whole thing in his mouth.

"Caden?"

He dragged his eyes up, lingering on that sexy chest hair and the tattoos inked into his skin. Fuck, he was so gorgeous. "Yeah?"

"Have you ever had sex before?" Quinten asked, holding his eyes.

He sank his teeth into his bottom lip and slowly shook his head.

Primal satisfaction flashed across Quinten's face, his fist squeezing the base of his cock. "Thank you for telling me," he rumbled, deep voice rolling over Caden.

Even through the heavy fog of arousal, the fact that he'd pleased Quinten was like a balloon full of helium in his chest, making him want to fly away.

"Lay down, kitten," he ordered quietly.

Sighing happily, he lowered himself back to the bed and widened his thighs.

"Perfect," Quinten murmured, palms sliding up the back of Caden's thighs and onto his ass cheeks.

He shivered at the compliment, then moaned when Quinten gave him a rough squeeze.

His whole body shuddered at his cheeks getting slowly pulled apart, exposing him fully. Wetness landed on his hole, and he jerked in surprise, then shuttled his hips forward a few times, humping helplessly at the mattress.

"Lie still."

He sucked in a breath and relaxed once more, tightening his muscles and whimpering when more spit hit him. "Quinten..."

"Shhh."

His thick, burning cock slapped between his cheeks, jolting him against the sheets.

"Goddess," he moaned, squeezing his eyes shut and fisting at the bedding. He held his breath, waiting to feel that broad head breach him, to feel so full and stretched and *taken*, but it didn't happen.

Quinten's big hands pushed his cheeks back together so that he could feel every inch pressing into his sensitive skin, and then he thrust.

"Oh!" he gasped, shocked at how good it felt.

"You like that?" Quinten asked, lowering himself until he was crushing Caden into the bed again. His hands landed on the back of Caden's, tangling their fingers together.

He pushed forward again, harder, so their skin slapped together, and Caden moaned long and loud.

He could hear the smug smile in Quinten's voice when he said, "Yeah you do. You love it."

All he could do was nod and try to take in everything: the heat from Quinten, causing sweat to begin to slick his skin; the scent of Quinten's arousal, sharp and so thick he could taste it as he panted helplessly beneath his bulk; the tight hold on his hands, keeping him still and exactly where Quinten wanted him; and the soft kisses raining down on his shoulders and neck interspersed with Quinten's deep grunts as he worked himself against Caden's body, using him to make himself feel good.

Of course he fucking loved it.

Quinten's thrusts sped up, the force driving Caden's weeping, neglected dick against the mattress over and over. Pleasure built inside him, filling every crack and crevice. Every inch of his skin felt overly sensitive, yet he craved more. More of Quinten's rough thrusts, more of his sweat-slicked skin, more of his callused hands squeezing his hands until his bones ached.

"Please..." He couldn't force out anything else, just repeated the word over and over, breathless and desperate.

"*Fuck*," Quinten grunted behind him, then his lips were right next to Caden's ear. "What do you want, kitten? You want to come? Or do you want me to spill all over this sexy ass and cover you in my scent?"

Caden cried out, his gut and balls tightening so hard and fast he thought he was going to release right then and there. "Yes, yes, yes. Quinten... please..."

"Please what?"

"Cover me," he gasped out, doing his best to push his ass back against Quinten, to offer as much of himself as he physically could. "Coat me in your scent. Own me."

Quinten groaned, long and low, and then Caden felt it as the scent of come hit his nose. Liquid heat landed on his low back, but then Quinten pulled his hips back and released one of Caden's hands.

Forcing his eyes open, Caden turned to look, chest heaving and dick aching, needing release, but he needed to see Quinten mark him more.

Teeth gritted, Quinten's fist shuttled up and down on his cock. His thick head was still wedged between Caden's cheeks, and he clenched, frantic to hold on to it. Quinten's brows furrowed in concentration, his next spurts of come landing directly on Caden's hole.

The sensation was overwhelming and devastating in the best way—he knew, down to the depths of his soul, he'd never want another man to mark him like this again.

Quinten was it.

His jaguar was purring in happiness, the sound so faint in the room he doubted Quinten could hear it over their heavy breathing. But it'd grow stronger as Caden recovered, and he wouldn't be able to hide his satisfaction.

Goddess, he didn't want to either. He wanted to revel in finding someone who saw him so clearly, who knew what he needed before he did.

Taking deep, ragged breaths, Quinten stared down at the mess he'd made for a moment, pure male satisfaction oozing out of him. Caden watched, completely captivated and trusting that Quinten wouldn't leave him on the edge.

Quinten ran his tongue over his top teeth. "You look well-used, kitten."

Caden whimpered.

Grinning, Quinten gripped his cheeks and spread him back open, humming appreciatively. "So beautiful."

He could only watch, transfixed, as Quinten rubbed his thumbs at the mess, inching closer to Caden's hole. Moaning, he pressed his face into the bed and pushed up, begging wordlessly for more.

Quinten's wet tongue licked up one of his cheeks just as he pushed a thumb coated in his come inside Caden. All the sensations, the knowledge of what Quinten was doing, threw him over the edge.

He cried out, voice muffled, as he squeezed down on that thick digit, wishing it was something bigger and longer but loving every second. Quinten pushed in harder before pulling down, stretching Caden's hole open.

Come shot out of him, his eyes rolling back in his head and every muscle tensing.

Quinten was murmuring something behind him, but he couldn't hear it over the blood rushing in his ears.

As soon as he finished coming, he flopped down, boneless.

Quinten chuckled. "You okay?"

"Killed me," he mumbled, eyes already closing. His body was heavy and pulsing with satisfaction.

"What a way to go," Quinten said softly, nuzzling into the back of Caden's neck. "At least roll out of the wet spot before you pass out."

"Can't..."

Just as sleep took him, he felt big, rough hands gently tugging at him.

Chapter Eleven

Quinten headed straight for the cup of French press coffee sitting on the butcher block island in his kitchen. Mrs. Burns always made it for him and had it ready at 7:45 whenever he was staying at the house. She knew his routine better than he did some days.

He was taking his first sip when he realized there was another silent presence in the room. He glanced over at Dare with his eyebrows raised.

The wolf's serious face was pinched with a frown, and then he inhaled exaggeratedly.

If Quinten wasn't who he was, he probably would've been embarrassed.

Fucking shifters with their damn noses.

It wasn't anything he wasn't used to, but it could still be aggravating. Hell, Liam used to make comments when Quinten was a teenager and couldn't keep his hand off his dick. He'd learned early you couldn't be around parahumans and maintain any sort of dignity.

"Is there something you want to say?" he asked Dare,

taking another sip of his glorious coffee. He wasn't sure what Mrs. Burns did to it, but it was always a little bit better than the housekeeper in his penthouse could do.

And ten times better than what he could do himself.

Dare still didn't say anything, just crossed his arms over his chest. The permanent sneer from his scar seemed deeper than normal.

"Don't be a judgy puppy," Quinten said. "He's a grown adult."

"He's vulnerable," Dare said in a low voice.

Quinten turned away and winced. Dare had him there.

It wasn't that it hadn't occurred to him last night. He just hadn't had the strength to push him away, not after what Caden had said. He wasn't sure why it had affected him so much, but the idea of a shifter who had three times his strength and speed could turn to him and feel safe and protected...

Intoxicating.

He knew Dare and the others felt comfortable around him, but it didn't extend to him physically protecting them. They could take care of themselves—and Caden could too. Maybe not at the moment because of the weakening from the collar, but he had lived his whole life not needing a human to keep him safe. But instead of turning to Dare or Nero, he'd crawled into Quinten's bed.

Then he'd whispered in the dark how safe Quinten made him feel, all while pressing his hot, silky skin against him.

He just couldn't resist.

It might make him a terrible, terrible person, but he found he didn't really give a shit. He had done far worse things in his life. Things that had left blood on his hands and enemies who held grudges.

Spending one night with his arms wrapped around Caden after making him feel good?

No, he couldn't regret that.

"ARE you going to come sit down?" Quinten asked with a smile.

Caden was busy looking through one of the bottom rows on a bookshelf all the way across the room. His sexy ass was up in the air, wiggling back and forth enticingly as he went along the spines.

When Quinten had found him earlier, he'd told him it was time for them to have a talk. He needed to know what had happened to Caden so he could be adequately prepared to protect him.

Caden had pouted, but Quinten held firm somehow, compromising by agreeing to have the conversation in the library instead of in his office.

"Just one second," Caden called, head still nearly touching the floor. Fuck, he was bendy. "I'm trying to find something Robbie told me about."

Quinten shook his head, but he wasn't really annoyed. He leaned back on the love seat he'd chosen from the small sitting area, prepared to wait as long as Caden needed to be ready. There were two bottles of water and a box of tissues on the table in the middle of the space.

Just in case.

The handful of things that Caden had said in passing over the last few days had hinted that there was more to his story than just getting captured and collared. That alone was traumatizing, especially with how close he'd come to dying.

It took nearly fifteen minutes before Caden finally wandered over toward him, and Quinten had to suppress a smile at the stack of three books cradled in his arms.

"You know, you don't have to take everything you want right now. You can come back later," Quinten said, remembering the large stack on the bedside table he'd spotted that morning. The books definitely hadn't been there before Caden's arrival, and for some reason, it had warmed his villainous heart to see them occupying the table on the side of the bed he never used.

"I don't want to forget," Caden said with a shrug.

Quinten stared at him for a second. "Why don't you just make a list on your phone?"

Blushing, Caden set the stack of books on the table next to the tissues and then sank into a chair across from him. "I don't have one."

Instead of asking why, he sighed and pulled out his own to send a text to Mrs. Burns. "There. It'll be here by this afternoon. We'll get you all set up."

"That's not necessary—"

Quinten cut him off. "It is necessary, and it's not a big deal. Don't fight me on this, kitten."

If anything, Caden blushed even more, though he wasn't sure if it was about getting the device or the endearment. Tucking his phone back in his pocket, Quinten relaxed again, keeping his posture open and nonthreatening.

Caden, on the other hand, was hunched over, hands twisting in his lap and eyes on the floor.

"Caden," Quinten said softly. "You don't have to be embarrassed about anything that happened."

"I know," Caden said. "It's just..."

Quinten didn't say anything, giving him space to organize his thoughts and to find his courage. He knew it was in there. Nobody could have survived whatever Caden had and not have been courageous, though he wondered if he didn't see it that way. If he'd had to do things to survive that made him feel cowardly.

"I should have seen it coming," Caden finally said. "Or at the very least not been so easily duped."

"Duped?"

"Yeah," Caden said, brows furrowing. He rubbed his palms on his jean-clad thighs and then raised his eyes and met Quinten's gaze. "I've been living pretty much as a nomad since I was fifteen."

Quinten leaned forward a little. "Fifteen? Were you traveling with your parents?"

Caden shook his head. "No, that's when they died."

"I'm so sorry."

"Thanks," Caden said with a little shrug, plucking at the bottom of his shirt. "It was a freak accident where their car got pinned under a semi. It took so long to extract them that not even their shifter healing could save them."

"Jesus," Quinten said softly. "That's fucking horrifying."

"Yeah. Took me a long time to feel comfortable in a car again," Caden said with a humorless laugh.

"Why did that turn you into a nomad?" Quinten wasn't exactly seeing the connection.

"The alpha in the pack we were living in... I didn't know him that well. It was a fairly large pack but not close-knit. Everyone just kind of did their own thing, you know?"

Quinten nodded but kept quiet, encouraging him to keep going.

"After they died, I went to talk to him. I wasn't sure what to do about the house, bills. I was so naïve. I just thought he'd direct me toward somebody in the pack to help take care of me. I was pretty much grown by then, but I was still in high school."

Quinten remembered what Liam was like at that age, and he couldn't help but disagree with the pretty much grown part. At fifteen, especially as a shifter, your life was a mess, no matter your family circumstances. The heightened senses added more hardships on top of the regular teenage angst.

Everyone around you was surging with hormones, distracting you. You were closed in a classroom with thirty people who couldn't control themselves, and yet you had to keep a part of yourself locked down tight.

It used to make Liam grumpy as hell. He'd come home in the evening with a headache and want nothing more than to flop down on top of Quinten and take a nap.

That Caden had been that age when he lost his parents and their grounding connection and managed to survive was impressive as hell.

The fact that he'd gone to his alpha for help and not gotten it was infuriating.

"He told me that he didn't abide by freeloaders in his pack," Caden said with a scowl, mimicking a deeper, more growly voice. "I told him I could get a job, but he said I wouldn't be able to earn enough to keep the house while I was in school, and he wasn't willing to take on a charity case."

"What a dick."

Caden must have been lost in his memories because he jumped in place a little, gaze darting up and a small smile creasing his face. "He really was. He tried to imply that there were... other things I could do to earn my keep."

Quinten's fists clenched. "He what?"

Caden shrugged. "Yeah. I don't know. It was kind of

weird. He wasn't really hitting on me, so I don't know if he meant, like, his Enforcers, but it was pretty heavily implied that I could stay at the alpha house if I was willing to do some... extracurricular things."

"That piece of shit," Quinten said through clenched teeth. He pulled out his phone. "What's his name? Where's this pack located?"

Caden's soft laugh drew his attention back up. "It's fine. You don't have to go into protective mode on him. It was a long time ago."

Quinten disagreed, but he decided not to push it since he knew there was a lot more to the story. He tucked his phone under his thigh and then spread his arms over the back of the loveseat. "So you left?"

Caden nodded. "I did. I guess I thought I could just find another pack, that someone would be willing to take me in. But more often than not, there was the same kind of mentality that I was too young to be able to earn my keep, that I didn't offer anything to the pack. So why should they waste resources on me?"

Quinten shook his head, wishing he was more surprised.

"When I was sixteen, I ended up with a couple of humans as foster parents. They were actually pretty nice, not abusive like you hear a lot about, but not super engaged. I don't know if it was because of my age, but they pretty much just let me do my own thing as long as I didn't cause too much trouble for them. They kept a roof over my head and food on the table in exchange. So I got a job and saved up some money. When I was eighteen, I bought this old Honda that I wasn't even sure would get me across the state line, but it did. It lasted for..."

Quinten studied his face. He wasn't sure what Caden

was thinking about, but he looked wistful. "How long did it last?"

Caden cleared his throat. "Last year, it finally died." He scrubbed at his face and shook out his arms before continuing. "I used it to drive around and visit different packs. I was pretty much over the idea of joining one for good after the shit I had gone through. I'd just stay for three to six months and then move on to the next place."

"Why didn't you just settle down outside of a pack?" Quinten asked.

"I'm not sure," Caden said slowly. "I had thought about it a couple of times, but..." He rubbed at his chest. "My jaguar was restless, driving me to move on like he was searching for something."

Quinten wanted to ask if his jaguar still felt that way, but then he'd have to punch himself in the face because he knew that was a loaded fucking question. Whatever was happening between them, it was temporary. It had to be.

Despite what had happened to him and what Caden had said, it was obvious he would thrive in a loving and supportive pack. One with a good alpha who didn't see the members as commodities or wastes of resources if they couldn't contribute enough.

Caden could never be truly happy with a packless human and a handful of shifters.

"So you kept moving," Quinten said softly.

"Yeah. I ended up settling with this pack down in Arkansas almost a year ago. It was mid-sized, which I preferred. The alpha was nice enough, so I stayed a little longer than I usually would." Caden hesitated, twisting his fingers in his lap. "A few months ago, I got invited to the alpha's house. It was strange but not completely unusual. It hadn't happened in that pack before, but other times, they would want to check in, see if I was planning on joining the

140

pack or would be moving on. This was a little different because I was invited for dinner."

His eyes were distant as he remembered what had happened. Quinten's gut started to twist, a bad feeling growing inside him.

"When I got there, the alpha was already sitting at the table with a couple of men I'd never met before. I was sure they weren't pack members."

"Shifters?" Quinten asked.

Caden nodded. "Yeah, one was a bear, and the other was a jackal."

Quinten raised his brows. Bears were a dime a dozen, but jackals were pretty rare. He tucked that bit of information away.

"I joined them, and dinner was served not long after. For a while, we just kind of chatted. Nothing important. The alpha didn't introduce the strangers to me, which seemed rude, but I just kept my head down, answered questions that were asked of me, and waited for it to be over."

"What kind of questions were they asking you?" Quinten interjected, already knowing the answer.

"Nothing suspicious," Caden said, shrugging. "The alpha asked how long I'd planned on staying, if I was considering joining, which was typical. They asked if I had family in the area or if something else had brought me there, how I was liking the pack, if I'd made any friends. Stuff like that."

Quinten cursed under his breath. "Goddammit."

Caden jerked his head up. "What?"

"Those weren't innocent questions, Caden."

"What do you mean?"

"They were trying to find out if you had ties to the area, if anyone would notice if you went missing."

The color drained from Caden's face. "Oh yeah, I guess

that makes sense." He shook his head. "Goddess, I can't believe I didn't figure that out before."

Quinten sighed. "It's my job to see the worst in people. You see the best. Don't feel bad about that."

Caden stared at him for a long time, not saying anything.

"Caden?"

He shook his head, glancing away. "Dinner was almost over, and I was relieved I would finally be able to leave. When one of the strangers got up and excused himself to go to the bathroom, I didn't think anything of it. I was so focused on the plate in front of me, of how uncomfortable the conversation was—the entire meal, really—that I didn't notice when he came back into the room. I definitely didn't notice when he came up behind me. I felt the smallest prick of pain in my neck, and that was it."

"They drugged you," Quinten verified.

"I guess? One minute, I was sitting at the table, and then next thing I knew, I was waking up somewhere I didn't recognize. It was like a jail cell, with a barred door and no windows. There was a tiny bunk bed, but nobody was ever in there with me. I-I was chained to the wall, but it was magicked so I couldn't break it." Caden's voice grew unsteady, and Quinten almost said they should take a break, but he plowed on before he could get the words out. "For a long time—it had to have been at least a week—nothing really happened. Somebody in a mask would walk past and slip some food through the door, and that was it. They didn't talk to me. They wouldn't tell me why I was there."

Jesus. That had to have been terrifying. Quinten focused on keeping his emotions locked down, not wanting to distract or make Caden feel worse. When he was alone, he'd let his rage boil over and beat the shit out of his heavy bag down in the gym.

"And every once in a while," Caden said, voice softer, "I would hear doors open, but I couldn't get close enough to mine because of the chain to see where they were or who was there. Sometimes at night, I'd hear people crying, but nobody answered when I called out." Caden smiled ruefully. "At first, I was frustrated. Why wouldn't they just answer me? But after I was there longer, I understood."

"Understood what?"

"There was no point in getting to know the other prisoners," Caden said, meeting his eyes. There was something incredibly sad in Caden's golden eyes, a devastating understanding most people would never have.

Not unless they'd stared death in the face and refused to blink.

"After the first week," he continued, rubbing at his short hair and leaving it disheveled, "they drugged my food, and I woke up in this room that was... I called it the Gray Room because that was all I could see while strapped to the table."

Quinten sucked in a breath. Tears glistened in Caden's eyes, but he kept going.

God, he was so fucking brave. His poor kitten.

"I could never see the faces of the guards when they brought the food, but the people who worked in that room... they didn't bother hiding."

"So you would recognize them?" Quinten asked, a thread of steel in his voice.

"Oh yeah," Caden said, huffing a sad little laugh. "I'll never forget their faces or scents. Or anything they did to me."

"Were they human?"

"Some, but the guards were all shifters. There was one Gray Room man who was a witch."

Quinten nodded, adding to his mental notes.

Sighing, Caden said, "I'm not sure what their goal was, but they were definitely experimenting."

Quinten's blood turned ice-cold. "Experimenting?"

"Yeah. They would in-inject me with stuff. Sometimes it would make me sick or make my blood burn so hot I thought I was on fire." He licked his lips, eyes distant and glassy. "Sometimes they wouldn't have an effect at all. Other times... Every once in a while, whatever concoction they put in me would force me to shift. But it was... wrong. It'd hurt so bad I'd pass out and then wake back up in my cell."

"I'm so sorry that happened to you," Quinten said, shaking his head. Some of the rumors he and his brother had been hearing about missing shifters were making more sense though.

Some sick fuckers were taking advantage of the fact there was no Council anymore, no Guardians yet, and no one watching out for parahumans.

Caden smiled sadly. "They weren't just experimenting on us. I would spend days going into the Gray Room, but then it would stop. The first time, I was so relieved, but I learned very fast I had no reason to be. Some of the guards would come to my cell with these long metal rods. One would have a metal collar attached to it, and they'd... they'd stick the rod through the bars and force it around my neck." He shook his head, hands fisted in his lap. "The cell was so small I couldn't get away. If I tried or resisted once it was on, the others would use their rods to electrocute me."

Quinten sucked in a breath, nostrils flaring. "Where did they take you?"

"The arena," Caden said, sighing heavily.

"The what?" Quinten leaned forward, bracing his fore-arms on his knees.

Caden matched his posture and nodded. "Like a gladi-

144

ator arena. That's what it looked like anyway. It was, like, this giant pit. The ground was covered in sand, and it was surrounded on all sides with twenty-foot walls that were so smooth not even a shifter could climb them. I-I saw a hawk shifter try to fly out once... She didn't make it. There was some sort of invisible netting over the whole thing. She got tangled in it and started screeching..."

Caden's breaths were coming fast, too fast. Quinten slid a hand onto the table between them, palm up, and he latched on, squeezing so tightly Quinten was sure he'd have bruises.

"The, uh, the audience didn't like it since it robbed them of the show they'd come to see."

"People were at the arena? Not just the guards?"

Caden shook his head. "The arena was always full of spectators. I couldn't see them well, and I didn't... I didn't like looking at them, but I think it was different people each time I was there."

Quinten didn't understand how he hadn't heard about something like this. Caden had said he'd been taken *months* ago, and he doubted he was the first one.

Just how long had this been going on? Since before the Council was taken out? Had they known about it? Was it another one of their dirty secrets?

It was too late to ask them, but Quinten had a few other unsavory characters he could apply some pressure to and get some fucking answers.

"So they made you fight each other," Quinten said, for some reason needing to hear Caden actually say the words to fully believe it.

Caden nodded miserably. "If we didn't... It was bad," he whispered. "The first time, I refused until I was nearly killed by the other shifter with me and was forced to defend myself. I couldn't blame him because I'm guessing he'd tried to resist, too, and faced the same consequences."

"What did they do?" Quinten seethed, blood boiling.

Caden's fingers twitched around Quinten's. "They... They didn't bring me any food for days, and then once I was weak enough, a bunch of the guards came into my cell. They had Tasers and baseball bats, but most just... punched and kicked. I-I don't know how many bones were broken before they stopped... but then they came back the next day... and then the next... Until finally someone from the Gray Room came and asked if I was going to behave. By then..."

When he didn't finish, Quinten gave his hand a squeeze in understanding. "You said yes to make it stop. Just like anyone would."

Tears were streaming down Caden's face. "I did. The next time they brought me into the arena, I fought. I fought as hard as I could. Usually, they'd let us stop once they'd gotten a good show and one of us yielded. But sometimes... You could tell when it was going to happen. The crowd would be louder than normal, really worked up. Those days... they'd make us keep going until... until one of us was dead."

He said the last word so softly Quinten almost didn't catch it.

"Jesus, kitten. That's so fucked-up. I'm so sorry they did that to you," Quinten said softly.

Caden's beautiful honey eyes met his, more tears streaming down his cheeks. "They made me kill people, Quinten. They turned me into a killer."

Quinten shook his head. "No, you're not. You're nothing of the sort. I know killers. Fuck, I am one." Caden stilled, watching him disbelievingly. "You were put in an incredibly tough situation, and you did what you had to do

146

to make it out the other side. They didn't turn you into anything. You're still just as sweet and kind as I'm sure you've always been."

Caden swiped at the wetness on his cheeks. He didn't agree or disagree with Quinten, but he took a deep, shaky breath and then exhaled it roughly. Some of the tension left his shoulders.

"After a few months, I just kind of figured they'd either get tired of doing their experiments or somebody would kill me in the arena," Caden said without any inflection to his voice, which was more terrifying than anything else he had said so far.

This sweet young man had accepted that he was going to die and there was nothing he could do about it. The toll that had to take on his psyche couldn't be measured.

"Then a few days ago, this guy came to my cell. He didn't wear a mask or dress like the Gray Room people did. I'd never seen him before. He was human but... scary."

"Scary how?" Quinten said, refocusing like a laser. That had to have been Tiho.

"The way he smiled at me," Caden said. "And the look in his eyes. I could just tell he enjoyed hurting people. He had this old guy with him, had to at least have been seventy, who smelled a little like magic. The older man pointed at me and said I was the one he'd seen, and the scary guy just grinned and told the guard with them that he'd take me."

Take him. Had they sold Caden to Tiho? Were they selling others, or had it been a one-time thing? Something Tiho had orchestrated with some of his daddy's money, maybe.

"What do you remember after that?" Quinten asked.

"They shot me with a tranquilizer, and when I woke up, I was in the warehouse. They had already chained me to the wall and collared me." Caden rubbed at his eyes with his free hand, the other still holding on to Quinten for dear life. "I was still a little groggy, but the scary guy knelt down right in front of my face, patted me on the cheek, and said that I shouldn't take it personally. It was just business."

Quinten bit back another curse. He was going to fucking rip Tiho Draža apart with his bare hands.

"He and the others left, and I tried to get the collar off or break the chain, but it just made the collar start to heat up. It was burning my skin, but the more I struggled, the worse it got until it became so excruciating I could barely think. I didn't know if anyone was going to find me. I didn't know if they were going to come back..."

"And then my people showed up," Quinten finished.

"Yeah, I didn't hurt any of them, right?"

Quinten shook his head quickly. "No, you didn't. Don't you remember?"

Caden shrugged. "Some of it, but some of it is kind of a blur. Like the pain short-circuited my brain, so I can't remember quite all of it. I remember a woman with a terrified face."

"That was Ginger."

"She wanted to help, but her mate kept her from getting too close. Which is probably for the best," Caden added with a sad smile. "If anyone had gotten close to me, I probably would've tried to hurt them. I was so scared."

His words ripped through Quinten's chest. "You didn't hurt anyone, and you didn't hurt me when I got close."

Caden stared at him, wide-eyed. "I don't even remember that. I remember seeing you. I remember your eyes, but I don't remember you getting close."

"After we broke the chain, you were in so much pain, just writhing on the floor. So I went over, put my hand on you, and I told you that you were going to be okay."

Caden's eyes widened even more. "Wait, I do remember

148

that. I remember hearing a voice say that right before I passed out, and it was the first time I believed it was going to actually be true."

"It is true," Quinten said, holding his gaze and gripping his hand as tightly as he could. "And it's going to stay true, kitten. I promise."

Chapter Twelve

"He's my new what now?"

Quinten opened his mouth to answer, but the grinning vampire beat him to it.

"Your new bodyguard."

That's what Caden had thought Quinten had said. He planted his hands on his hips. "I don't need a bodyguard."

Quinten squeezed the bridge of his nose. "He's not..." He stopped and took a quick breath. "He's just a little added protection while we figure out if Tiho is going to slink off or if he's going to make another move against us."

Caden frowned at him. He had thought things were okay between them after he told Quinten what happened to him. It had been difficult to say the words, but he'd actually felt better after he had told his story, like the weight of it wasn't sitting on his chest anymore.

But last night, Quinten hadn't come to bed.

Caden had stayed up as late as he could, but he'd been exhausted after reliving everything and ended up falling asleep. He'd assumed that when he woke up, Quinten would be there. But he hadn't been, and he'd barely seen him all day today, skipping all of the meals and then calling Caden into his office like he was just another employee.

And now a bodyguard. It was hard not to feel like Quinten saw him differently, like he was too weak to protect himself, and while that hurt, it also pissed him off. He was already feeling stronger. Each day, his jaguar was growing more and more restless, wanting to be free. Waiting the whole week to be able to shift was going to suck, but there was no doubt in his mind that when the time came, he'd be able to do it.

Despite what Kai and the others had said, healing at Quinten's house without a strong pack around him was going just fine. He glanced at the wolf and vampire flanking either side of Quinten.

Well, without an *official* pack.

Crossing his arms over his chest, he lifted his chin. "You know I can protect myself, right? Despite what happened to me, I'm strong and fast, and I know how to fight."

Quinten's face softened, and he started to take a step forward but stopped himself. Instead, he leaned back against the front of his desk, clasping his hands on the edge until his knuckles were white.

"I'm not saying you aren't. I know you can protect yourself. But we don't know who else Tiho has working with him other than the seer. That alone gives him an advantage." He nodded his head toward Nero. "Vampires are just as fast and strong as shifters, and their sense of smell is even better than a wolf's. He's just going to be sticking close to make sure that you're okay."

"No one even knows we're here, do they?" Caden asked.

"Not necessarily, but again, if the seer is powerful enough, it's possible that they know exactly where we are, and since Dare and I have to make a trip into the city in the next few days…"

Caden straightened. He hadn't heard anything about that. Why would they be going into the city? That sounded like they were leaving him behind.

"I don't want you unprotected while we're gone."

"Robbie stays here without protection." He did his best not to jut his lip, but he was feeling rejected after Quinten had avoided him last night and today.

Quinten might say he still saw him the same, but it didn't feel that way.

"No one knows Robbie's here," Quinten said, beginning to sound frustrated. "They don't even know he exists. If anyone saw him coming in and out of the house, they would assume he was an employee. They have no way of knowing who he is to me, and while the same goes for you, Tiho is different. His seer already has his sights on you. We don't know if he's going to try and come after you again. Until we do—until he's handled—Nero is sticking with you."

"But—"

"Caden, this isn't up for discussion."

Clenching his jaw, Caden twisted around and stormed out of the office. He pretended he didn't notice the vampire following him. He headed straight for his favorite place in the whole house and slammed the door to the library behind him, breathing heavily.

He didn't hear it open or close again when Nero let himself in, but he could feel him.

"I'm perfectly safe in here."

"I know. I just thought we could talk."

"About what?" He whipped around and glared at the vampire. "About how you think I'm a weakling, too, and need protection?"

For the first time since Caden had met him, Nero

looked pissed. "That's not what's happening. You need to get that shit out of your head."

"Well then, why is Quinten—"

"Because he protects what's his." Nero said it emphatically, holding Caden's gaze. "You hear me?"

Caden ran his teeth over his bottom lip. Yeah, he heard him, and he'd heard Quinten say that the first night he met him.

But... it didn't feel like it was true for him. It felt like Quinten was putting distance between them for some reason, so the show of concern for his well-being felt out of place, almost condescending.

If it had happened two days ago, he would have loved it. It would have made him feel protected and safe, even if he didn't really need it. He'd know it was just Quinten's way of showing how much he cared. He wrapped his arms around himself and tried to hold on to his glare as he met Nero's sky-blue eyes.

"He says that, but he's being weird."

Nero strolled over to the same love seat Quinten had sat on the day before. The reminder made his chest ache. He should have edited some of it out. He'd just meant to tell him the highlights but had ended up word vomiting the entire thing. But it had been like lancing a wound. He'd needed to apply the red-hot poker to where it was festering so that it could start to heal. Except now he was left in limbo, not even sure how long he'd be welcome there. Once he proved he was healed and shifted, would they ask him to leave?

"Come sit, kid."

"I'm not a kid," he said but went over and plopped down on one of the soft leather chairs.

"How old are you?"

He shrugged. "Twenty-three."

Nero laughed. "You're a kid to me." He leaned forward and braced his elbows on his thighs, propping his head up on his clasped hands. "I know you've lived a rough life, and I know you've seen things and been places, so you think you know what's what," Nero said, watching Caden steadily. "But that doesn't mean you have all of the answers. Don't assume shit. Definitely don't assume anything when it comes to Quinten."

Caden narrowed his eyes. "What do you mean?"

Nero tilted his head. "I know the Kincaids talked to you about him."

"Yeah," he said with a shrug. "Kai tried to tell me I should stay there, but he didn't really go into detail because Dare was in the room."

"But then right before you left?"

Caden widened his eyes. He hadn't realized anyone knew. "How did you find out?"

Nero smiled wider. "Parahumans forget that just because Quinten doesn't have enhanced senses doesn't mean he doesn't know tricks. While a lot of times shifters—" He shrugged. "Okay, and vampires. We can get lazy and depend on our sense of smell or hearing too much. Quinten doesn't trust anyone, and he doesn't simply rely on his senses to know information."

"What does that mean?" Caden narrowed his eyes.

Chuckling, Nero said, "It means he planted a bug."

"A bug?" Caden furrowed his brows. "What kind of bug?"

"The listening device kind. He slipped it into your pocket before he got pulled away by Rick, and it wasn't affected by Gabriel's little hex bag."

"He did?" He'd no idea. Quinten hadn't said a thing about it.

"Of course he did. He knew they would probably try

155

something like that. So he knows what Gabriel said to you."

"It doesn't matter to me," Caden said, waving a hand in the air. "It's not like I think he's some saint. I know he does things that other people think are questionable or unethical."

"And?"

Caden shrugged. "And nothing. It doesn't matter to me."

"Why?"

"Because..."

He wasn't sure how to explain it, and he wasn't even sure he *wanted* to explain it to this guy he didn't know very well. Though he supposed they'd get plenty of chances to get to know each other now.

"Because I trust him. I don't have to know him well to know that my instincts are always right. Well, usually right," he said and smiled ruefully. "Besides, most of what Gabriel told me were rumors. People say this. People have heard that. Even though Gabriel has known him for years, he doesn't know exactly what Quinten does. As far as I'm concerned, anything Quinten wants to share with me is great, but I'm not going to trust some rumor from someone I don't know over a man who let me into his home with no questions asked, saved my life by cashing in a favor with the most powerful man on the continent, and has asked for nothing in return. He's earned the benefit of the doubt as far as I'm concerned."

Nero nodded. "That's a good answer. I'll leave it to him to share how much of those rumors are true then." He pushed to his feet. "But remember what I said. Don't assume anything about him. Don't get pissed at him because he wants to protect you. It doesn't mean he sees you as weak. Dare follows him everywhere. Do you think that makes Quinten weak?"

156

"Well, no, but he is a human."

Nero smiled, but it wasn't quite as nice as before. There was a little bit of fang showing, his eyes hard. "He is. But again, appearances aren't always what they seem."

CADEN TOSSED and turned in bed for what felt like hours until he finally threw back the sheets and climbed out of bed. He was tired of this.

It was the second night in a row Quinten hadn't come to his own bedroom to sleep. If he wanted Caden to leave, he should have just said so. He had thought what they'd shared in his bed had been special and that maybe it was the beginning of something, something more than just Caden needing a place to stay to get better.

But maybe he was wrong.

He'd heard what Nero had said that evening though, and he'd decided to go to the source instead of assuming the worst. If Quinten wanted him out of his bed, then he could damn well say it. He wasn't a child. He didn't need to be coddled.

He didn't even bother putting on clothes before he stormed out of the bedroom. He lifted his head into the air and inhaled deeply. The scent of orange blossoms led him down several hallways to a bedroom that was farthest in the house from the master.

He stood outside the closed door, fighting back tears.

He'd hoped he would find Quinten working in his office. Instead, he was in another bedroom in his own home, hiding from Caden. Taking a deep breath, he braced himself and pushed open the door.

Despite the late hour, Quinten was sitting up in bed with a lamp turned on next to him, casually reading a book.

The blankets were down around his waist, showing off his bare torso and that chest hair that Caden wanted to burrow inside of. It was unfair how attractive the man was.

He crossed his arms over his chest. "What are you doing in here?"

Quinten had the good grace to wince, looking a little guilty. "I just thought it would be easier if I slept in here."

"You thought it would be easier if you slept in a room other than your bedroom?"

"Caden..."

"No. Explain it to me, Quinten. Hell, maybe explain it to me like I'm a child because it sure seems like you didn't want to sleep with me anymore, but rather than just saying that, you found the bedroom the farthest you could possibly get from me and just avoided it."

Quinten threw back the covers, setting his book down on the table next to him, not bothering to mark the page. He was wearing nothing but black boxer briefs that would have normally made Caden drool. But the way he was holding his hands up, like Caden was some wild animal, pissed him off more.

He stormed across the room. "Just say it, Quinten. I'm not going to run away and put myself in danger if you tell me you don't want to have sex with me. That didn't have to happen again. It's just comforting having another person nearby. Someone I trust."

Quinten cupped the sides of his face. "I don't regret what happened between us. But after what you told me yesterday—"

Caden flinched. He knew it. He knew it had changed the way Quinten had looked at him.

"No. Stop." Quinten tightened his grip on his face. "After what you told me, it felt like I had taken advantage of you."

158

"Like you had forced me?" How had Caden begging for it come off like he'd been forced?

"Well, no, but you're so much younger than I am, and you've just gone through this terrible thing. There's a power imbalance, kitten."

"So..." Caden squinted at him. "You think that I'm so immature and traumatized I don't know what I want?"

Quinten's jaw tightened. "That's not exactly what I meant."

"Well, it sure sounded like it. But I'm not a cub, and I'm not curled up in the corner, too afraid of shadows to move. Yes, what happened to me sucked. It still sucks. I woke up screaming again last night, except you weren't there this time to comfort me. You were too busy hiding from me, worried that the big bad mobster was taking advantage of me."

Quinten's eyes began to heat, his thumbs caressing against Caden's cheekbones. "I don't want you to look back at what happened in this house and regret anything."

Caden was on the edge of a precipice. He could turn back, or he could jump.

He might fall... or he might fly.

"The only thing I'd regret," he said softly, "is not getting to be with you."

Quinten sucked in a breath, his nostrils flaring, and then he was crushing his lips against Caden's for the first time.

Whimpering, Caden grabbed onto his forearms and held on for dear life.

Goddess, the man could kiss.

His lips moved insistently, his tongue swiping at Caden's mouth until he opened on a groan, and Quinten dove in, tasting every inch of him. His fingers tightened on Caden's jaw, the tiny lick of pain shooting fire through his veins.

The soft, scratchiness of Quinten's beard made him shudder, and he pressed closer, needing so much more.

Quinten's mouth slid away, latching onto Caden's neck. He threw his head back on a hoarse moan, his hands scrambling for purchase on the smooth skin of Quinten's back.

"Fuck, kitten, I love the sounds you make. So fucking needy for me."

Shivering, he nodded loosely, barely keeping his legs under him as Quinten sucked hard on the side of his neck. He keened softly, arching his whole body and rubbing their growing erections together.

"What do you want?" Quinten mumbled, moving down to Caden's shoulder and biting down.

His body jolted, the tip of his cock beginning to leak already.

It took barely anything for this man to get him so riled up he was worried he'd start humping his thigh to get relief. He knew why though, even if Quinten couldn't see it yet.

They were perfect for each other because they were made for one another.

His human instinctively knew exactly how to touch him, when to be rough and when to be soft. How to drive him wild with just a few words.

"Kitten?"

"Hmm?" He threaded his fingers through Quinten's soft hair, encouraging him to keep licking and biting at the sensitive skin of his throat.

"What do you want?" he asked again, amusement clear in his voice.

"Whatever you want," he said, breathless and without hesitation.

Quinten groaned, nipped at the edge of his jaw, and lifted his head. "Fuck, you already look wrecked."

Caden just nodded, too distracted by Quinten's lust-filled hazel eyes and damp lips to really focus on what he was saying. He supposed that probably did mean he was wrecked. Wholly, completely. Smashed to pieces by this man who so many feared but whom Caden trusted with every part of himself.

"Get on your knees, kitten."

Moaning, Caden dropped to the hard floor in an instant, reaching out and grabbing the back of Quinten's thighs and staring up at him. His thick chest was heaving, and his cock was rock-hard behind the thin material of his briefs.

Caden's mouth watered as he stared at it, wanting it in his mouth more than he wanted his next breath.

"God, look at you," Quinten grunted, hooking his thumbs into the waistband and pushing them down. They got caught on his thick, hairy thighs, so Caden snagged the bunched-up material and tugged them the rest of the way down.

Then he leaned in and buried his face in the crease between Quinten's thigh and groin.

He moaned at the heady scent of orange blossoms and sweat, unable to resist licking Quinten's heavy-hanging balls.

Rough fingers sank into his hair and held him tighter against that fragrant skin, pressing him so close he could barely breathe.

He loved it. It was as close as he'd ever get to sinking inside Quinten's scent and skin, and he *reveled* in it, loving how Quinten was taking control but still giving him what he wanted.

He used his tongue to draw one ball into his mouth, sucking on it gently. He groaned in disappointment when those strong fingers yanked him back. Licking his lips, he could still taste Quinten's salty skin on them and shivered.

Quinten tilted his head back, tracing Caden's mouth

with one of his fingers. "You're going to look so gorgeous with my cock in here."

Arousal surged through him so hard and fast he felt his eyes begin to glow and his teeth start to sharpen.

Quinten tsked teasingly. "No fangs, kitten."

"Sorry," he murmured. Swallowing, he concentrated for a second until they were back to normal, then opened his mouth to show he was ready.

Groaning, Quinten pushed two fingers inside, rubbing them against his tongue. He moaned, automatically closing around them and sucking.

"So eager," Quinten said, his deep voice little more than a rumble that cascaded over Caden's skin. He slipped his fingers free and grabbed the base of his cock, pointing the broad head at Caden, but his grip in his hair held him in place. "You ready?"

He sucked his lower lip into his mouth, staring at the dripping tip right in front of him. The scent was over-whelming, wrapping around him and making him light-headed. "Yes, Quin."

Grinning ferally, Quinten closed the last few inches between them until his weeping head was brushing against Caden's lips. He painted his precome across Caden's bottom one, and he moaned, licking at it and then Quinten's slit, lapping up as much as he could get.

"Open for me, Caden. Show me how well you can suck me."

He opened wide, holding still as Quinten fed him his cock.

"Good," Quinten murmured. "Now, suck."

Caden closed his lips around him and hollowed his cheeks, his eyes rolling back in his head at the musky taste so bright and strong on his tongue. He tried to hold still, to let Quinten lead, but he wanted more, he wanted all of it.

Quinten's hold tightened in his hair, shooting little jolts of electricity down his scalp and spine until they settled in his balls, and he moaned around his mouthful.

"That's it, kitten." He pulled out until only the head was still inside, then pushed forward, giving Caden even more. Quinten moaned and did it again. "Look at me, Caden."

It took effort for him to focus his eyes, but he did it, slurping on Quinten's cock as he met his fiery gaze.

"Fuck," he grunted, hips slamming forward and making Caden gag. "Shit, sorry."

Caden shook his head as best he could, holding on to the back of Quinten's thighs. He didn't want sorry; he wanted to be used. For Quinten to get himself off and own Caden in the process.

"We'll have to work on your gag reflex," Quinten said, shallowing his thrusts despite Caden's desire to choke on him. "I bet you'll love to practice, won't you?"

He had an image of himself on his knees under Quinten's desk, practicing not gagging on his big cock as Quinten conducted business above him.

Whimpering, he tried to nod.

Quinten hummed and picked up his pace, using his grip on Caden to pull him forward at the same time he sank back in. "Fuck yeah, you will. My good kitten. You're going to live to suck my dick, aren't you?"

Caden's eyes rolled back, and his hips punched forward, come shooting out of his untouched cock. He screamed around Quinten as wave after wave of pleasure crashed through him.

He heard Quinten swear above him, but he couldn't focus, could barely keep himself upright.

"Suck on the tip," he grunted, and somehow, Caden complied even as he listed a little to the side.

He heard the wet sound of Quinten's fist stroke himself furiously, and then his essence was filling Caden's mouth, spurting onto his tongue and drowning him in his flavor. Moaning, he sucked at him greedily, wanting every last drop.

He zoned out for a bit and only came around when Quinten eased his fully softened cock from his suckling lips. Gently, Quinten stroked his head and tipped his face up.

"You were perfect, kitten."

Tears filled his eyes, warmth flooding him. Sucking in a hiccupping breath, he leaned into Quinten, wrapping his arms around his hips and holding tight.

Quinten just kept stroking his hair and ears, scratching lightly at his nape. In no hurry at all.

Once his breathing evened out and his tears stopped, Caden opened his eyes and stared at the tattoo of the red rose on Quinten's hip. He traced the outline, smiling when Quinten shivered.

"What's it mean?" he whispered. He knew it had to have a special meaning to his human; it was different from the rest of the ink on his body. It was the only tattoo with color, yeah, but it was also beautiful where most of the rest seemed perfunctory.

"It's a reminder."

"Of what?" It was probably rude to ask, but he didn't want any secrets between him and Quinten, not even something little.

"No matter how dark the world gets, there's still beauty. Sometimes it's just hidden."

His eyes stung again, but he blinked the tears away. "I love that." He placed a soft kiss to the center of the rose, then climbed to his feet. "What about this one?"

Quinten looked down at where Caden was tracing the infinity symbol beneath the word *Amato*.

He snorted a laugh, drawing Caden's eyes to his face. "Liam's idea. He got one just like it and pestered me until I'd get one to match. A symbol of our brotherly bond."

He said it laughingly but with such fondness Caden's heart swelled in his chest. "That's sweet."

"I don't know about that, but I finally gave in after my dad died."

"I'm sorry. When was that?"

"Almost five years ago."

Caden cocked his head, studying his wonderfully complex human. "Why did that convince you?"

"Because I found out the real reason he got his," he said, smiling. "He got drunk on shifter wine and told me how he wanted to be an Amato forever, not just because our parents were married. I think that little shit actually thought I wouldn't consider us family anymore once we weren't connected by their mating. I got the tattoo the next morning while he was still nursing his hangover."

"You," Caden said, clasping the sides of Quinten's face, "are so soft and mushy on the inside, aren't you?"

Quinten scoffed. "Hardly."

"Mhm." He knew better. He'd just need to convince him to see himself how Caden did.

Oh, and ease him into the fact that they were fated mates.

One step at a time though.

"You're done here, right?" Caden asked, glancing at the room around them.

"Yeah, kitten."

"Good. You don't sleep anywhere but next to me from now on, Quinten Amato. I won't have it."

Grinning, Quinten wrapped his arms around Caden and palmed his ass cheeks. "Yes, kitten."

Chapter Thirteen

"We're at a dead end," Dom said, sighing. "Ash has tapped all his sources, and I've gone back to some of mine, but no one knows where Tiho is hiding out. Is it possible he left town?"

Quinten leaned back in his desk chair. It had been almost two weeks since his phone call with Tiho, and he supposed it was possible the fucker had taken his warnings to heart, but his instincts were saying differently.

"It is, but I don't buy it."

"Yeah, me either," Dom said glumly. "At least Vlatko is toeing the line."

Quinten grinned. That was putting it mildly. He and Dare had flown into the city for a meeting with the new head of the Borko family a week ago, and Vlat had fallen all over himself to make it clear he had nothing to do with his brother, had sent down the word that Tiho was being denounced, and would cooperate any way he could moving forward.

Quinten gave it two years before he owned Vlatko and ran the crime family himself.

"Any word on Tiho's mom? Dare will be pissed if I don't ask."

Dom chuckled. "Of course he will. I did finally track her down to a cemetery on the south side of the city. Looks like she died of an *indeterminate cause* when her sweet Tihomir was seventeen."

"That's not suspicious," he mumbled, pulling his emails up on his computer and scrolling through to see if anything urgent had come through.

"Right? Not surprising though, considering how long it took to find her and the shit we've uncovered about Tiho."

A few days ago, Dom had gotten his hands on an unsealed copy of Tiho's juvenile criminal record. There hadn't been anything they hadn't suspected, but the animal mutilations and fires pretty much confirmed what they'd already known.

"How much longer will you guys be staying out there?" Dom asked. "Ginger has a new spell she wants to try on you."

Quinten laughed. "Your wife is a little twisted."

"You have no idea," he said adoringly.

"We probably won't stay too much longer. It's been nice having the time with Robbie, but he's gone to Vegas for the week. Plus, being away from some of the bullshit that gets thrown at me when I'm there has been a relief, but I can't indefinitely run things from here. I think my assistant at AI is about to quit."

"The one who leaves her desk whenever you walk by?"

"Different one. That one didn't last six weeks. This one won't last another month." He sighed. "She hides behind her computer screen when I come out of my office, Dom. What am I supposed to do with that?"

He snorted. "You should just hire someone from the pack and stop messing around with these timid humans."

168

"We don't—" He cut himself off, not bothering to correct him. "You know I like to keep that side of things parahuman-free."

"Yeah, and I think it's dumb, but it's your call."

"Thanks for your honesty," he said dryly.

"No problem, boss! See you soon, hopefully."

"See you soon."

He laid his phone on his desk and went back to his emails, wanting to be finished by the time Caden, Dare, and Nero got back from their run. The three went into the woods behind his house at least once a day, Dare and Caden shifting, and ran for an hour or two. Caden—and Dare after Caden left his office—assured Quinten repeatedly that he was feeling as strong as ever, but the first time, he was pretty sure everyone had been holding their breath as Caden slowly but gracefully changed forms.

Each time after, he'd gotten faster until he could do it in just a second or two. Even Dare was impressed at how fast he could change, though he'd only expressed it with a twitch of his eyebrows.

He got sucked into work, losing track of time. His office door slowly swinging open drew his eyes up, and he grinned at the enormous jaguar prowling toward him, eyes glowing a bright gold.

"There's my sweet kitten."

Caden opened his impressive jaws, flashing him his long fangs and giving a quick barking roar of displeasure. While in his jaguar form, he didn't appreciate being called *kitten* as much.

"I know, I know. You're a big, ferocious cat." He turned his chair to meet him as he came around Quinten's desk. His back nearly reached the top, but he kept his head lowered, stalking forward.

God, he was gorgeous. His orangish-tan snout was the

169

only area he didn't have spots, the tip of his nose black like his markings. His small, rounded ears had adorable tufts of fur on the inside that were incredibly ticklish, and his black-tipped tail flicked back and forth when he was annoyed.

"Did you guys have fun?" He leaned over, extending his hand but waiting for Caden before touching him. Sometimes he didn't like being petted and would dart away, but most of the time, he craved the touches.

Sure enough, his big, soft head pushed into Quinten's palm, demanding scritches.

A loud, steady purring filled the room as soon as he complied, bringing up both hands to give attention to his jowls and around his ears.

Before too long, Caden was pushing into his body, trying to get closer. He was sure that if he could have, he would have climbed right into Quinten's lap for a cuddle.

"Do you want to go upstairs and nap like this? I can bring my laptop."

He stared at Caden's bare skin a few seconds later, his cock thickening in his slacks. There was always a wildness about Caden when he got back from a run as his cat, a predatory gleam in his eyes, the scent of sunshine and leaves clinging to his skin.

"No, I don't want a nap," Caden said lowly, climbing into Quinten's lap and straddling his thighs. He sank his fingers in Quinten's hair, tugging his head back a little rougher than he normally would, and licked up the side of his neck, stopping for a second to suck on his earlobe.

Quinten took a shuddery breath, hands spanning Caden's sun-warmed low back. "Does my kitten need something?"

An animalistic growl right in his ear should not have been a fucking turn-on.

And yet...

170

"You, Quin. I need you. No more teasing."

Quinten turned and pressed his smile into Caden's messy hair. "I haven't been teasing you—"

"Yes, you have! For weeks, you've refused to fuck me, and I can't take it anymore."

Grabbing some of Caden's hair, he jerked his head back, humor gone. "I've been preparing you, not refusing. We're not in a rush here, Caden."

Caden rolled his eyes, his irises still glowing softly. "I'm in a rush. I feel like I'm going to crawl out of my skin if I don't get you inside me."

Heat crawled down Quinten's spine. "I've been inside you."

"Your fingers," Caden grumbled, like he didn't go off like a damn geyser every time.

"And my tongue."

Pink washed over Caden's cheeks, and Quinten couldn't stop himself from leaning in and tasting the color. "Okay, yes, but I'm ready for your cock. I promise I'm ready."

He'd known for days Caden was getting impatient, but Quinten kept holding him off, knowing that as soon as they crossed that line, things would be... different. It wasn't that he didn't want Caden—fucking hell, did he ever—but he knew what it would mean for the cat. He'd seen the looks Caden had been giving him when he thought Quinten wasn't looking; he'd noticed how obsessive he'd gotten about getting Quinten's scent all over him and his mouth on the curve of his neck, right where a bonding bite would go.

Except Quinten's useless human teeth couldn't give him that.

And it wasn't the only thing Quinten couldn't give him.

"Quin," Caden moaned, rubbing his whole body against him. "Please."

171

His control snapped. He'd probably hate himself one day when his heart was ripped from his chest the day Caden left him to get the things he needed from someone who could actually give them to him.

But today...

Today, he'd make Caden his.

He ran his hands down the supple muscles of Caden's back and to his strong thighs, loving how much he'd filled out in just two weeks, but it also meant there was no way he and his nearly forty-year-old back could carry him up the stairs, even if Caden did the heavy lifting by holding on to him with his arms and legs.

"Okay, kitten. Let's go upstairs."

Caden moaned in relief and jumped up, but he didn't hurry out of the room. Instead, he hopped up onto Quinten's desk and spread his legs.

"No, here."

Quinten stood, rearranging himself in his pants, and glanced at the open door behind Caden. "You deserve a bed—"

"I want this," he said clearly, grabbing the front of Quinten's button-up shirt and tugging him between his legs. "You're a fucking king, Quinten. Fuck me in your throne room."

This man was going to kill him.

He had his tongue shoved down Caden's throat before he could even draw his next breath, holding him tight just like his jaguar craved, his fingers digging in just behind Caden's sensitive ears.

He devoured him.

They were so close, their bodies entwined and souls fucking touching, that he nearly lost his head and forgot about the door.

He tried to pull back, but Caden's hands held him tight.

"The door," he managed to say, his voice muffled against the side of Caden's mouth.

"Leave it," Caden moaned, wrapping his legs around Quinten and biting at his throat.

His hips jerked forward involuntarily. "People will—"

"Let them," Caden hissed, pushing back against his cock. He pressed a kiss to the skin he'd just bitten, then leaned back until he was lying on Quinten's desk. His long cock was flushed a deep red already, the tip damp, and his chest heaved. He held Quinten's eyes with his glowing gaze. "Let them hear, Quin. They should know how a king owns his property."

Jesus fuck. He was going to come in his damn shorts if Caden kept that up.

"My kinky little kitten," he said, shaking his head and planting his hands on either side of him. He hovered above Caden, staring for a second at his gorgeous, flushed face and thanking whatever deity brought this man into his life. "You'll have to let me go so I can get undressed and find some lube."

He patted one of Caden's thighs, but his hold only tightened around his hips. "Leave the clothes," he said, sinking his teeth into his bottom lip. "And I snuck some into the top drawer earlier."

So, this was a planned seduction.

Well played.

He jerked the drawer open and found the half-full bottle of lube that used to be in his shower. Setting it on the desktop, he held Caden's eyes as he slipped off his cuff links, then slowly and deliberately rolled his sleeves up to his elbows.

Caden licked his lips, eyes glued to the smallest strip-tease known to man.

"Put your feet on the desk," he ordered, picking the bottle back up and wetting two of his fingers.

Moaning, Caden finally relaxed his thighs and pulled his knees up to plant his feet on the edge of the desk.

"Spread them wider, kitten. Show me what's mine."

Caden's whole body undulated, his arms flying up above his head to grab at the opposite edge and feet sliding apart to open himself to Quinten.

"Beautiful," he murmured, slipping his wet fingers between Caden's cheeks and circling his hole.

Caden arched against him, pushing back to try and get him inside. He slumped back in frustration when Quinten simply pulled his fingers back. "Quin..."

"Yes, kitten?"

"You're teasing again."

"Maybe a little." Then, he sank them both in at once, pure satisfaction thumping through him at the way Caden threw his head back and cried out. His walls clenched around his fingers, trying to hold him when he drew them back before pushing in once more.

"Oh goddess," Caden moaned, tossing his head.

Quinten smirked, crooked his fingers, and rubbed right over Caden's highly sensitive prostate.

If the whole house hadn't already known what they were doing, the scream Caden released clued them in. Surprisingly, the idea didn't bother him. It wasn't like the parahumans in the house wouldn't have been able to hear them if they'd gone upstairs, though it was polite to tune out those kinds of things.

But the fact that they'd deliberately left the door open, sending a clear message to anyone within hearing distance that Caden was his and he satisfied the hell out of him, made his chest swell with pride.

"More, Quin, please. I need more. Need you," Caden

174

begged, scrambling for purchase against the smooth top of his desk.

"I know. I've got you."

He pulled his fingers out slowly, spreading Caden wide as he went and making him groan. Once he was free of his tempting heat, Quinten grabbed the lube again and slicked his weeping cock.

Caden was nodding, fast and loose, his glowing, hooded eyes watching him raptly.

"Yes, fuck yes. Give me that cock. Fill me up and wreck me, Quin. Do it, please."

He gritted his teeth, his balls tightening at the string of crude words falling from Caden's lips. His cat was a quick study, picking up Quinten's dirty talk and running with it, knowing it drove him just as crazy as it did Caden when he did it.

Lining up, he pushed steadily until his head popped in past the first ring of muscle, both of them groaning. Caden was so damn hot inside, his walls silky smooth and clinging to Quinten perfectly.

"Fuck, you're taking it so well, kitten." Quinten pushed in slowly but without hesitation. He watched Caden's eyes widen as his hole stretched to take the thickest part of his shaft. "Halfway there."

"Halfway? Goddess, you really are going to wreck me."

Quinten laughed breathlessly, leaning over until he was only a few inches from Caden's wonder-filled face. "That's the fucking plan."

Then, he thrust the rest of the way in and held as Caden wailed and grabbed at his shoulders, his legs wrapping around his waist. His insides fluttered around Quinten, and he had to squeeze his eyes shut and breathe for a second to stop himself from going off immediately.

"You're so tight, kitten." He grunted as Caden squeezed

down on him. "Jesus, do that again. Fuck yeah, squeeze that dick."

Caden moaned and rocked against him, fucking massaging Quinten's cock with his pulsing walls.

He couldn't hold still any longer, the need to thrust and claim this man overpowering him. Slowly, he pulled his whole length out.

"What? No," Caden cried.

Quinten drove back inside, jaw set in concentration.

Caden keened. "*Yes*. Yes, yes, yes. Harder, please."

He gave him harder, bracing himself as best he could on the slippery desk and just railing into him. The sound of their skin slapping together melded with the never-ending sounds of pleasure rolling from Caden. It drove Quinten mad, his strokes becoming less rhythmic and more erratic as he chased his and Caden's pleasure.

He was watching his cat through sex-hazed eyes, running his gaze over every inch he could see. When he met Caden's glowing eyes as he neared the point of no return, Caden held him captive, then tipped his head back and turned his chin to the side.

Exposing his neck. Submitting to Quinten.

Snarling, Quinten lunged forward and wrapped his fingers around that delectable column. Caden moaned and went lax, his body only moving because of how hard Quinten was thrusting into him.

"You're mine, aren't you?" he said, whispering the words into Caden's ear and then tugging the lobe into his mouth and sucking.

"Yes," Caden moaned and let his arms fall to the desk, giving himself completely over to Quinten. "I'm yours."

"I know, kitten. I've always known. Ever since you crawled in my bed and begged me to cover you in my scent."

176

Caden shuddered beneath him. They were pressed so close together he could feel Caden's cock pulsing where it was trapped between them, rubbing against Quinten's skin every time he thrust.

Tightening his grip on Caden's throat, he murmured, "My perfect cock-slut of a kitten," and then bit his neck, right where it met his shoulder. Where his bonding bite would go.

Caden's shout had an edge of a roar to it, making Quinten's ears ring. He held on with his teeth as he rutted into Caden, prolonging his orgasm and chasing his own.

Flinging his arms around Quinten, Caden arched his back and tightened around him. Quinten grunted and drove forward as far as he could, holding himself as deep inside Caden as he could get, and came.

Caden moaned and flopped back down on the desk, his legs falling away and his fingers tracing up and down Quinten's back as he caught his breath. Quinten panted into his neck, giving a few more thrusts, his instincts driving him to push his release as deep as possible inside his ma—

He froze, his wet dick still inside Caden's body, and silently called himself every kind of name imaginable. God, he'd thought Caden would be the one to...

This was bad. He should have never—

No, he couldn't even be sorry, even if his instincts were completely wrong. He'd just need to put up some boundaries, make sure things didn't go any further, and keep Caden from—

"Love you, mate," Caden mumbled sleepily, his breaths deepening and body completely relaxing under him.

Fuck.

Chapter Fourteen

He'd fucked everything up.

Caden cast a glance over at Quinten where he sat on the other side of the back seat of the SUV, head dipped as he studied something on his phone. He'd barely said two words to Caden all day.

After rousing Caden from where he'd fallen asleep on his desk the night before, they'd stumbled up to bed together and fallen asleep. Everything had seemed so perfect.

But when Caden had woken up and reached for his mate, the other side of the bed had been cold.

It wasn't completely unheard of for Quinten to get up without waking him, though he usually did when he gave him a kiss before heading down to his office, and Caden just fell back to sleep after.

Ignoring the stone growing in his gut, he'd gone down to find Quinten wasn't actually in the house. Nero had told him that he and Dare had gone to meet with someone and would be back later.

It had been harder to ignore the pitying look on the vampire's face.

Well after he'd eaten dinner alone, Robbie still off having fun with his friends, Quinten finally came home, but he'd brushed Caden off, heading into his office with his phone pressed to his ear.

Caden had stared after him, heart in his stomach.

An hour ago, Nero had found him in the library and told him he needed to pack. He'd smiled, calling it a surprise trip to see Quinten's brother, but there had been a sour edge of dishonesty in his scent.

But when he'd gotten into the SUV and found Quinten, he'd asked where they were going, and he'd said the same thing: "Going to see my brother. You'll like him."

There had been no lie in his scent or heartbeat, so Caden had told himself he'd imagined it with Nero. Except... Quinten hadn't said much else to him during the ride to the private airfield, and when he'd asked Nero how long they'd be gone for, Nero had looked away and told him he wasn't sure. To just pack everything he had.

Everything he had. For a last-minute, surprise trip to Kansas to visit Quinten's brother.

Nope, nothing disconcerting about that at all.

The fact that Quinten had been in the car when Caden had climbed inside had been a little bit of a surprise, and he felt terrible about it. He'd had himself convinced that Quinten had gotten so freaked-out by what Caden had said the night before that he was shipping him off somewhere.

He'd been ridiculously relieved to see him sitting there in his pristine suit, salt-and-pepper hair neat and pushed back from his face.

Of course, he wasn't going to just ship him off.

Sure, Quinten hadn't said he loved him back, but he'd called Caden his. He'd called him his and bitten him right where a shifter would to bond them together. That had to mean something.

Maybe it was too fast by human standards, and he wasn't ready to say it back, but Caden knew Quinten cared about him. Things had been incredible between them the last couple of weeks.

And yet... Quinten wouldn't even look at him now.

Yeah, he'd definitely fucked things up. He just hoped Quinten would get over his freak-out soon.

He chanced another quick glance over at Quinten. If he was... done with Caden, would he be taking a trip with him, introducing him to his family?

Maybe he just didn't know how to express his feelings. He'd overheard him tell his brother that he loved him, but he'd known Liam since he was a child. Maybe he didn't know how to tell a partner.

They both knew of plenty of mate pairings that were made up of parahumans and humans, so he couldn't imagine that was the issue. And they'd gotten past the whole "taking advantage" thing weeks ago.

They'd been *happy*.

He was sure of it.

When Quinten had gone into the city the week before, he'd come back less than thirty-six hours after he left. Yet when he'd come into their bedroom, he'd been ravenous, grabbing ahold of Caden and kissing him like they'd been separated for months and not hours.

He couldn't imagine how that didn't mean what he thought it meant.

Quinten would figure out they were made for one another. He just needed to be patient.

The private airfield was small, with only a couple of hangars, and there didn't seem to be anybody else around. As they pulled up to a waiting jet, their driver, Alan, stepped out of the SUV, going around toward the back.

Caden put his hand on the door handle, prepared to

exit as well, but Quinten hadn't moved. Dare was in the front passenger seat, and he glanced back for a second, but he didn't say anything before climbing out.

Frustrated, Caden said, "Are you going to stare at your phone this whole trip, or will I be getting the pleasure of your company at some point?"

Quinten raised his head and gave him a distracted smile that didn't quite reach his eyes. "I'm just trying to answer a few emails before we get in the air. You understand."

He was already looking back down at the device before he finished talking, so he didn't see the way Caden's eyebrows practically hit his hairline.

You understand?

No, he didn't fucking understand. He didn't understand what was happening *at all*. The fact that people were waiting on them to get on this plane was the only thing that stopped him from demanding answers. He would wait until they were stuck a few thousand feet in the air and then tell Quinten to just spit it out and explain what had him acting so weird.

If he needed time to get used to the fact they were mates, that was fine. If he needed longer to come to terms with his feelings for Caden, that was fine too.

But he couldn't just shut down every time he felt a strong emotion.

Huffing, Caden wrenched open the door, got out, and slammed it behind him. He sent an apologetic look toward Alan when he stared at Caden in shock.

"Sorry."

Alan smiled and reached into the SUV to grab Caden's suitcase—well, Quinten's suitcase full of the clothes Quinten's housekeeper had bought him.

"Oh, I can get that. You can grab Quin's since he'll be a few minutes."

Alan paused, looked at Dare where he was leaning against the back of the vehicle, and then gave Caden a more forced smile. "I've got it. No worries."

Caden stared after him, wondering why everyone around him was acting insane. He turned back to find Dare watching him, jaw clenched and lips pressed so tightly together they were stark white.

"What's wrong?"

Dare just shook his head. Stepping closer, he clasped the side of Caden's neck for the first time, scenting him like a packmate, then turned and stormed away, heading into the open hangar.

"Um. Okay..." Seriously, had they all been hit with a strangeness spell or something?

He walked around to the back to grab Quinten's stuff to help out Alan and found the space empty.

He frowned. There was no way Alan had had enough time to bring Quinten's suitcase to the plane and come back to get Caden's before he'd gotten out of the car.

Which meant...

Caden stared at the plane, the pieces of the puzzle finally sliding together.

He'd been right after all.

He'd thought that because Quinten was in the SUV, that meant he was coming with him, that they were taking the trip *together*, but he hadn't packed a single item. He obviously planned on flying down, saying hello to his brother, and then coming right back.

But Caden wasn't.

Caden had been told to pack for an indefinite length of time. To bring everything he had.

Did the man honestly expect him to stay behind with his brother—an alpha he didn't know—and his pack of feline shifters just because he said so?

His heart breaking, he tried to focus on the anger surging through him instead.

As he stomped around the SUV, Nero pulled in behind them in a separate vehicle, a couple of extra shifters with him.

Caden wasn't sure why Quinten had bothered to bring so much manpower, but then again, maybe he wasn't flying to his brother's. Maybe that had been a lie, and Caden had just been too love-blind to see it.

He pulled open the door, and Quinten looked up at him distractedly. "I'm almost done."

"I don't care," Caden said, voice wavering. "Why don't you have any bags?"

Quinten stared at him for a long moment and then ran his tongue over his teeth. "I won't be staying very long."

Caden nodded. "Yeah, that's what I thought. So are you..." He shook his head, blinking quickly to try and get rid of his tears before they could fall. "Are you just getting rid of me or what?"

Quinten slid out of the SUV, and for the first time since he'd woken up in his penthouse, Caden put space between them, stepping back so that they wouldn't touch.

He frowned, but he didn't move closer. "It's not forever. Once we're sure that Tiho isn't a problem anymore—"

Caden didn't let him finish, laughing humorlessly. "Save it."

"Caden—"

"No, be quiet, Quinten. Goddess, I thought we were past this." He rubbed his face, pretending they didn't come away wet. "How can you be so strong and yet such a coward?"

Quinten reared back like he'd been struck.

Caden didn't let him say anything, pressing on. "If you just wanted me to leave, you should have just said so. I thought I made that clear last time. I don't know why you don't feel the same draw that my jaguar and I do, but I wouldn't have made it hard on you."

"Listen, Caden—"

He cut him off again. He couldn't listen to some excuse about how Caden deserved better, or Quinten was too old for him, or whatever it was he'd convinced himself made them not right for one another.

"I get it. You don't have to explain. You're done. All the things you've said, what happened in your office yesterday—none of them meant anything to you. Not like they did to me." Caden flicked at the tears starting to fall, frustrated with himself for being unable to stop them.

Quinten made a pissed-off noise and then grabbed Caden's arm, tugging him toward the plane.

"Where are we going? I'm not flying to Kansas with you," Caden said, but he didn't pull his arm away.

Quinten didn't answer, simply dragging him up the stairs and into the luxurious private jet.

"Everyone get the fuck off," he barked, and the flight attendant and pilot ran off the plane like it was on fire.

"Quinten, that was rude." His breath froze in his throat when Quinten turned on him, face furious.

"I never said those things didn't mean anything to me. Do not put words in my mouth."

Caden licked his lips and stepped back, but Quinten just kept coming, crowding him into a seat and then looming over him.

"It's obvious," Caden shot back, holding on to his anger as best he could. "You didn't mean it, and then you freaked out when I told you I loved you. Message received." He licked at his lips, unable to look away from Quinten's hot glare. "No offense to your brother—I'm sure his pack is great

185

—but I'm not going there. I've been fine on my own for years. I can do it again."

Quinten planted his hands on the armrests of the seat Caden was trapped in and leaned down so their faces were only inches apart. "You can't just take off, not while there's a threat hanging over your head. You're going to go to Kansas, and you're going to stay with Liam until it's taken care of, and Nero's going with you."

Caden stared up into the face that he adored more than any other, tracing the line of his jaw covered in the short beard he loved to rub his face against, up to his thick brows and into his salt-and-pepper hair, and then back down to his hazel eyes. They were so captivating. Even when his face showed nothing else, his eyes never lied.

Except they had, hadn't they?

Every time they had been together, every time Quinten had touched Caden and called him perfect and beautiful and *his*, his eyes had lied about what he was feeling, about the connection they were building.

Swallowing, Caden tipped his head back defiantly. "Yeah, I'm going to pass."

One of Quinten's hands shot up, his fingers wrapping around his throat just like it had yesterday in his office. His hold was firm and possessive but not too tight. Just like yesterday, Caden's whole body heated with excitement, his jaguar rumbling inside him, ready to show his belly.

He'd loved this side of his mate, but the reminder of what they had shared and how little it had apparently meant to Quinten was like a dagger to his heart.

"Now is not the time to be a brat, kitten."

Caden sucked in a breath, tears streaming down his face. "I'm so sorry that I'm not making your life easier as you break my fucking heart," he yelled sarcastically.

Quinten's fingers flexed against his throat, his eyes

186

burning. Caden wanted to look away, needed to if he wanted to preserve a shed of his heart, but he couldn't. He was wholly ensnared by this stubborn, complicated human.

Quinten pressed in close and rubbed his lips against the side of Caden's face. "That's the last thing I want." Before Caden could get his hopes up, Quinten continued. "But you need a real mate and a pack. Things I can't give you."

His chest rose and fell quickly as he struggled to catch his breath. Gathering his strength, he grabbed Quinten's wrist and pulled him away, slipping past him to stand a few feet away.

His skin already felt cold without his mate's touch.

"You're such an idiot," he said, shaking his head. "I have a pack." He stepped closer and stared into Quinten's confused eyes. "*You* have a pack. It doesn't matter that you're human. None of them care. All of the important things that make up a pack, you have that. You just need to get your head out of your ass and accept it."

Quinten's mouth opened and closed a couple of times, but no words came out.

Caden started to turn, ready to be off that plane before he did something he'd regret, but he paused to look back at him. "And if I didn't love you so fucking much, I'd punch you in the face for saying that you weren't my real mate."

Chapter Fifteen

Quinten watched Caden leave the plane, and it felt like his heart physically ripped its way out of his chest to follow him.

He rubbed the space between his pecs as he sank into the seat Caden had been in just a moment before. How had he fucked things up so completely?

Oh, that's right, because he was a coward, just like Caden had said.

Why was he fighting this? Why was he trying to make them both miserable?

He'd been so focused on trying to find the threat against Caden, against himself, that he'd pushed everything else aside. Nothing else had seemed as important, but Caden had been right.

He was scared.

The only person he'd let himself truly love that he wasn't related to by blood was Liam, and he hadn't even let himself be introduced to that little shit for a year.

But he'd fallen so hard, so fast as soon as he did. He would do anything for his brother.

Literally anything.

If he called him and said he had a body to bury, Quinten would fly down to help without a single question asked.

Okay, well, he'd send Dare down to help. Moving a dead body sounded like sweaty work and not something he wanted to do in his suits.

Either way, there wasn't a single thing he wouldn't do for or give his brother. His love for him was as absolute as his love for his son or parents.

But he'd never thought he would feel that way about anybody else.

The life he lived, the things that he saw and had to do, it wasn't safe.

That was why he'd sent Liam away. It was why he kept Robbie hidden.

And yet... he'd walked into that warehouse two weeks ago, found a naked man chained to the wall, and felt his entire life turn upside down.

He hadn't spent so long away from the city in years. People kept asking him when he was going to be coming back. He was sure there were rumors that he'd been injured or even killed since the only time he'd been back was for his meeting with Vlatko, and he'd flown back right afterward. Otherwise, he'd been conducting his business quietly, as far removed from the chaos of the city as possible, and it wasn't even just because Caden had needed peace and quiet to heal.

He'd just been enjoying it.

Enjoying the time they were spending together, the time he was getting with his son. Relaxing in the evenings with Caden curled up next to him as they watched trashy TV instead of forcing himself to make appearances at events he didn't care about.

It had been... nice.

And rather than ask himself why he'd been putting off going back to his real life, he'd shoved it down, ignored it, pretended that it was for Caden's safety.

As if his penthouse—in a building full of his people— wasn't three times as secure.

He pushed to his feet.

He had to make this right. The idea of losing Caden was far more terrifying than the idea of loving him. It had been shitty and selfish of him to think that he could just pack him up and ship him off, make him his brother's problem while Quinten avoided dealing with his own issues.

He started toward the door and stopped. Caden needed space. His jaguar needed to run, Quinten could tell. He'd seen it a few times the last couple of weeks, where Caden would get too antsy or worked up about something, and the only thing that helped was shifting and sprinting through the woods or zigzagging through the hedge maze.

He'd even jumped into the pool once and swam around before flopping onto his side on the heated cement and napping for an hour.

Liam had always been the same. He'd never noticed if some of the other shifters had the same sort of traits, but he figured it was definitely a cat thing at the very least. They just got grumpy and frustrated if they didn't stretch their fur often enough.

Instead of tracking him down and forcing him to have a conversation, he pulled out his phone and texted Nero.

Quinten: *Make sure that Caden gets back to the house. Dare and I are going into the city for the night, but I'll be back tomorrow.*

Nero texted back quickly. *It didn't sound like he wanted to go back to the house, boss.*

Quinten swallowed. He'd known that they'd all be able to hear, even as he'd dragged Caden into the plane. But for the first time in a long time, a spike of rage shot through him at the lack of privacy.

Quinten: *I didn't ask for your opinion. If he's not at the house in the next hour, I'm holding you personally responsible.*

Nero: *Understood, sir.*

Usually, Nero's texts were filled with emojis and LOLs. He knew he had pissed him off with his half-thought-out plan. Dare had been upset the entire drive to the airport too. Quinten figured he probably owed them an apology for forcing them to go along with hurting Caden.

But at the moment, he was just exhausted.

All he wanted was to wrap his arms around his kitten and have him forgive him. He had a hard time seeing what kind of future they could have together, but he knew he had to be a part of it.

And not on the periphery, like he kept his brother and son, but firmly entrenched in it, getting his hands dirty, standing by Quinten's side.

That was what he wanted, and if he had gotten to know Caden as well as he thought the last couple of weeks, he knew that was the kind of mate Caden would be.

He just... God, he was terrified he wouldn't be enough. That he'd fall short in giving his jaguar all the things he needed from a mate.

He made his way off the plane and back to the SUV. Alan was waiting next to it, prepared to drive him back to the house or take care of the SUV.

"I'm going to fly to the city in the helicopter. Thanks for the ride."

He patted Alan on the shoulder as he passed and then

headed into the hangar, where he'd seen Dare storm off to before Caden had confronted him.

He found the sour wolf going through one of the storage lockers they kept there. He was fairly certain everything in there was already well organized, but it was something Dare did when he was upset.

"I'm going to text Arnold. He should be here soon."

"Already did," Dare said without turning around.

"Dare."

The wolf whipped around. "Don't."

It was all he said before he marched out of the hangar. Quinten rubbed at his forehead, wondering if there was anybody else in his life he could piss off.

His phone started to ring. A bit of brotherly premonition told him that his day was about to get a smidge worse. Sure enough, he pulled it out to find Liam's name on the screen. He almost didn't answer, knowing he was about to get an earful. But he deserved to know that they weren't coming anymore.

"Hey," he answered.

"Hey, yourself," Liam said. "What's this I hear about you fucking everything up?"

He wasn't sure which one of his people had texted his brother, but they were getting fired immediately.

"I miscalculated," he said lowly.

"No shit. I told you that you couldn't just bring somebody to a new pack and drop them off. These things are delicate."

Quinten rolled his eyes. "Yes, and like I told you, he'd be the perfect fit for your pack."

"Brother, I hate to tell you this, but you're a dumbass."

"Liam."

"No, seriously. The kid already has a pack, the one his mate runs." He said it slowly, like Quinten was a small child who couldn't understand big words. "Now, are you done sticking your head in the sand and pretending like that isn't the reality? The fact is, I know you sent me away to try and protect me. I understood. I've always understood. So does Robbie."

He swallowed, his heart starting to race in his chest.

"But the reason I *had* to leave was because you were right. I needed to be an alpha to my own pack since the one I was living in already had one."

Quinten turned to face the wall and closed his eyes, letting his brother's words sink into his skin.

"I couldn't stand in your shadow anymore. It was time that I found my own place in the world."

"I'm so proud of you for doing it, you know," Quinten couldn't help but say.

"I know, but it's time you stepped out of the shadows too, Q. The world is changing, and it's time that you make a place for yourself in it. One front and center, not scurrying around in the dark like the boogeyman."

"I have a lot of enemies," Quinten muttered, though he didn't necessarily disagree.

If his trip to the Kincaid Pack had shown him anything, it was that it might be more valuable to have packs like that as allies rather than adversaries. The things that he did for packs and covens he'd had to start doing because of who the Council was and what they did.

But now that they were gone...

He sighed heavily. "He's really pissed at me."

"Of course he is," Liam said. "You shoved your entire leg in your mouth."

He chuckled. "Fuck, I miss you."

"Well, how about next time you guys actually come for a visit and not for a drop-and-run."

"Drop-and-run?" Quinten asked.

"You know, sort of like a hit-and-run, only instead, you drop a person off someplace they don't want to be, and then you leave them there and run away."

"You think you're so funny, cub."

"I'm hilarious. Now, go fix things with your mate."

Then, his brother hung up on him. Little shit.

BY THE TIME they landed on the roof of Quinten's high-rise, he was just about done with Dare's stony silence. The thing was, he was almost positive he wasn't just offended on Caden's behalf. He was pretty sure he'd hurt *Dare's* feelings.

Dare had called their tight-knit group a pack more times than he could count, and Quinten had always shrugged it off. But when he denied it as a reason for trying to distance himself from his mate, it hurt him.

Like he'd always figured Quinten would come around but saying it to Caden made his denial more real.

They stepped into the elevator, and Quinten pressed the button for the penthouse floor, Dare pressing the one for his own, just beneath the communal space below Quinten's.

"Dare," he started.

He kept his face forward, arms crossed over his chest. "Don't worry about it. Do you need anything tonight?"

He held back a sigh. "No. You can go check on everyone if you want."

Checking on everyone who lived in the building was something Dare always did when they returned from staying outside the city or got back from a business trip. He wouldn't be able to settle in his own apartment until he put eyes on everyone.

Dare nodded as the elevator dinged and the doors

opened. Quinten stepped out, but before the doors could close, he put a hand on them to keep them open.

"For what it's worth, I know I was wrong."

Dare met his eyes for the first time in hours.

"You guys are right. I didn't want to believe it, and I kept saying it wasn't true, but that doesn't mean it isn't. Caden and Liam are right. You were right. I need to get over my own insecurities and accept that even if I never dreamed of this or wanted the responsibility, I have it. I owe you all better than to continue to deny it."

Dare didn't say anything, but Quinten had known him for over a decade. He could tell that he was affected by his words, his face and stance softening just a touch, and then he nodded. "Apology accepted."

Quinten snorted and let the elevator doors close.

As soon as he stepped into the penthouse, he could feel that there was something off, a sinister tension to the air. He flicked on the lights and started moving through the place, and it didn't take long before he found the man dressed in black waiting in his living room, a glass of one of his bottles of wine sitting on the table in front of him, half-drank.

"By all means, make yourself at home," Quinten said, narrowing his eyes.

"Thank you. I have been."

"Tiho, I presume?"

"At your service," Tiho said, lifting the gun in his hand to salute Quinten sarcastically.

Two more men stepped out of the shadows, and as Quinten watched, their eyes began to glow, and their teeth lengthened.

"You know," Tiho said, leaning forward to grab the glass and take another sip, "your security is a lot less *tight* when you're not in this building. Did you know that?"

Quinten didn't respond, just shrugged out of his suit

jacket and tossed it over the back of a chair before unknotting his tie.

"It's true," Tiho continued the conversation without him. "I thought I would have to try and hit you at that country house of yours. Very swanky, by the way."

Quinten clenched his teeth.

"But then a friend of mine helped me see that this place would be the best opportunity."

"Is that friend of yours a seer?" Quinten asked, glancing around his apartment. "Is he here right now?"

Tiho waved the gun at him. "Oh, no. He doesn't really get out that much. Arthritis."

He said it with a wince, like he actually gave a shit about the guy, but Quinten had known a psychopath or two in his day, and he could tell it was all fake. He had a feeling most everything about Tiho was fake, except for the gun in his hand and the shifters standing behind him.

"But he did tell me that you'd be arriving here tonight all by your lonesome, no shifter friends with you."

Quinten nodded slowly, rolling up his tie and setting it on top of his suit jacket. "I see, and what is it exactly that you felt the need to break into my home to say?"

"Say?" Tiho repeated. "Oh, nothing really. But I did come to kill you. That was pretty much the only reason."

Quinten undid one of his cuff links and dropped it in his pants pocket, folding back the sleeve. "I see. May I ask why?"

"Sure," Tiho said cheerfully. "So you know how my dad died?"

"You mean how you killed him."

"Tomatoes, tomatoes," Tiho said. "The point is, after he died, I thought I would finally be able to move up in the family business. But Vlatko, well, he was as much of a tight-ass as the old man was. He said that I couldn't be trusted, murderous tendencies, blah, blah, blah."

Quinten popped out his other cuff link, palming it before rolling up his other sleeve. "Well, I can see how your brother might feel that way."

"Oh, because of this?" Tiho said, waving his gun in the air and then pointing at the shifters behind him. "Yeah. I didn't say he was wrong. But it is annoying, and the fact of the matter is I'm a Borko too. Even if my slut mom gave me her name instead of his."

"You didn't really answer my question," Quinten said.

"Hm? Oh, right. So. Killing you is going to make me look really good because there's a lot of people who talk behind Vlatko's back—and they used to behind Dad's too—about how weak it made them look that they had this agreement with you, almost like they were scared to go up against you. But me? I'm not scared. You might be surrounded by shifters and witches and all this magic bullshit, but you? You're just some human. Some mobster who thinks that because he's got magic at his beck and call, that makes him fucking special. But we know the truth, don't we?" Tiho said, leaning over like he was sharing a secret. "There's nothing special about you, only the people you surround yourself with. But once you're gone, they'll scatter. It's in their nature."

The shifters behind him cocked their heads but didn't say anything. Quinten wondered if they knew just how crazy their boss was. It didn't matter though. They'd die just the same.

"You know," Quinten said, pushing the tip of his thumb against the edge of his cuff link, "people have called me a lot of things in my life. Gangster. Don. Mobster. They've said a lot of things about me. But you know what they should have been calling me?"

Tiho cocked his head, eyebrows raised like he was actually interested.

"Alpha."

Quinten sliced his thumb open on the cuff link that had been specifically made for just that purpose.

"What the hell?" one of the shifters said, catching the scent of blood in the air.

Quinten pressed his blood onto the runes tattooed on the inside of his left arm, making sure to cover all three.

As soon as he pressed the last one, heat raced through him, enveloping his entire body. Power unlike anything he'd ever felt before surged inside him, looking for release.

He lifted his head and locked his eyes on Tiho, who was gaping at him. He cocked his head, a sour scent hitting his nose and making his mouth water.

"But you're—"

Quinten attacked.

Chapter Sixteen

"If I were smarter, I'd stop loving him."

Nero snorted next to him in the car. "Trust me. If it worked that way, I'd have done it years ago."

Caden jerked his head around and stared at the vampire. "Wait, what? Who are you in love with?"

Nero pulled his thumb and finger across his lips. "Not telling."

"Yeah, fine. Keep your secrets." Caden slumped in the passenger seat.

They were almost to the penthouse, and he still wasn't sure what he was going to say, other than maybe call Quinten an idiot again. After their confrontation on the plane, he'd shifted and run for almost an hour, all through the cornfields surrounding the airport.

When he'd finally calmed down and felt like he could have a conversation with Quinten without either punching him in the face or breaking down in tears, he'd returned only to find that his mate had just flown off in the helicopter to go into the city for the night.

He'd barely even gotten the words out to tell Nero that that was where they were going then, and the vampire had stomped on the gas. It had taken him a little while to get used to just how fast he could drive. But luckily, they both could hear police radios long before they came into range of their speed traps.

He looked at the city flying past them. "I don't actually want to stop loving him," he said softly.

"I know, kid," Nero said. "You don't have to either. Sometimes, the boss man just takes a while to come around to an idea. If you hadn't noticed, he can be a touch stubborn."

"Quinten? No," Caden said sarcastically. "But you're right. I moved too fast. It's like, even though I know he's human, I still want to do things at the speed that I would if he were a shifter, and that's not fair for him."

Nero shrugged. "I think that this has more to do with his stuff than anything else."

Caden looked at him. "You think so?"

"Definitely. He tries to hide it. But sometimes, I think he still feels like that little boy whose family got broken up because his dad left his mom for a shifter."

Caden sat up straighter. "He'd mentioned that his parents got divorced and that's how he and Liam became stepbrothers."

Nero laughed lightly. "Yeah, it was a little more traumatic than that. I wasn't around then. Well, I hadn't met Quinten by then. He was just a kid, after all."

"Wait, how old are you," Caden interrupted.

But Nero just waved him off. "But from what I've pieced together over the years, Quinten basically felt passed over for a newer, better son who had all of these special gifts that Quinten could never compete with. So as he'd grown up, he decided to prove that he didn't need those special gifts, that he could be just as powerful as a human."

"That makes sense," Caden said slowly, "considering

what he does and the kind of side business dealings that he has."

Nero nodded. "Yeah, I think he's more than proved to himself that he's good enough, but none of us ever truly outgrow our childhoods, do we?"

He glanced down at where Caden was squeezing his seat and had been for the entire trip. Even though he hadn't said anything or asked Nero to slow down, he knew that was true. He'd never completely get over his fear of cars because of how his parents died.

He could only imagine what it had been like for Quinten. To have his family broken up one day and to feel like he could never be good enough for his dad's new family. He doubted that was his dad's intent, but sometimes, feelings didn't make sense. They definitely weren't logical most of the time.

It made him so sad to think that even a small part of Quinten still felt like that little boy, like there was any way he wasn't good enough or strong enough for Caden.

As soon as he was done lecturing his mate on staying and talking and not running away in a helicopter, he was going to give him the biggest fucking hug.

Nero said they were two minutes out still, but a second later, Caden gasped and clutched at his chest. He'd just felt the strangest sensation, like a tugging behind his ribs.

Nero grunted next to him, and when he glanced over, his eyes were glowing a faint red. "Did you just feel that?"

"Yeah," Caden said, nodding. "What the hell was that?"

"I think I know, and I don't like it."

Somehow, he went the last few blocks through city traffic even faster, whipping into the garage underneath the high-rise and not even bothering to turn the car off before they were sprinting out to the elevator.

Caden hit the button, but Nero grabbed his arm and

dragged him farther down the wall. "We can take the express one. Goes straight to the penthouse."

"Thank fuck."

They still had to wait for it to come down, but as soon as the doors opened, they leapt inside and hit the button to take them up. They flew up the dozens of floors, but it still seemed like they were crawling. The sensation in his chest had faded, but he could tell something was off. He just knew it was Quinten, that he was in trouble. Maybe even hurt.

Nero had his phone out, and he was trying to call Quinten and then Dare and then Quinten again, but neither answered. As soon as the elevator doors opened, they ran forward, Caden skidding to a halt just inside the penthouse's living room.

He stared wide-eyed at where Dare was half-shifted and fighting a fully shifted cougar. But that wasn't what made his heart jump into his throat. On the other side of the room, over by the floor-to-ceiling windows, was Quinten fighting a shifted panther, whose pitch-black fur eerily melded with the dark floor.

He started forward when the panther crouched, about to strike, but Quinten caught him in midair and threw him to the ground. He was facing where Caden was standing, and he gasped.

Quinten's eyes were *glowing*, and his teeth were sharp-looking. Not as long as a shifter's or vampire's fangs would be, but definitely deadlier than they normally were. The runes tattooed on the inside of his left forearm were glowing, and there was blood smeared on them. He could taste it on the back of his tongue.

He didn't know what was happening, but Nero darted forward to help Quinten finish off the panther. Caden turned to check on Dare and caught movement in the corner of the room.

There he was, the man who had taken him from his prison, only to lock him in a collar that almost killed him.

Instead of smiling gleefully like he had been the last time, he was screaming orders, spit flying from his mouth and gun waving in the air. "Kill him! Kill him already!"

Caden was moving before he even realized it, leaping over furniture and heading straight for him. The man lifted his gun as he caught sight of him, eyes widening.

He leapt just as the gun went off, but he ignored the sting in his hip and landed on the human, knocking the weapon away and pressing his claws into his very vulnerable throat.

"Don't fucking move," he hissed in the man's face.

"You're not supposed to be here," he said furiously. "He said you wouldn't be here."

"Well, I am. You just tried to kill my mate."

"This is all wrong!" Tiho screamed, thumping his fists on the ground like a toddler having a tantrum.

Caden ignored him, turning to check on the others.

Dare was moving toward him, the cougar's body shifting back into human behind him. Quinten was also on his way over, eyes still glowing, as Nero held the panther—still in his shifted form—around the chest and sank his long, razor-sharp teeth into his furry neck from behind.

The panther roared in pain and outrage, but Nero just drank furiously, his eyes glowing red-hot like the embers of a fire.

Quinten was panting as he dropped onto the floor next to Caden. "I've got it from here. You can move back," he said softly, meeting Caden's gaze.

"No, he deserves to die. I have to kill him," Caden said.

205

His fingers twitched, but he couldn't make himself sink his claws into his throat, not now that he was unarmed.

All of the shifters he'd been forced to kill flashed in front of his eyes, but it wasn't the same. This man deserved it! He'd tried to kill him and then just tried to kill his mate!

Why couldn't Caden just do it?

He didn't realize he was crying until Quinten cupped his chin and raised his face, soothingly wiping away the wetness. "You don't need to kill him, kitten, but he does deserve to die."

He licked his lips and stared at Quinten. "You shouldn't have to."

Quinten shook his head, stopping him. "You hated killing, but it's something I've grown... accustomed to over the years. Let me do this for you."

Caden swallowed and backed up, keeping most of his weight on Tiho's legs so he couldn't get up.

Dare moved closer. "I can do it."

But Quinten shook his head, taking Caden's place. He pinned Tiho to the ground with one hand on his chest. "No, this is my kill. You've been living on borrowed time, Tiho," he said, almost soothingly. "Ever since you laid hands on my mate, you had to know this day would come."

"This isn't over—" Tiho started to say, but Quinten didn't let him.

His fingers, tipped with long claws, sliced through his throat. Blood sprayed all over him and Tiho.

"Couldn't have just broken his neck, huh," Dare said dryly.

For some reason, that set Caden off to laughing, the reminder of the first time he'd been in the penthouse and watched Dare kill someone. Quinten had made the same complaint.

He laughed and laughed until the humor turned to

relieved, gasping sobs, and then Quinten's arms were around him.

He stank of blood, but there were still orange blossoms underneath, so he buried his face in his neck and just breathed.

Chapter Seventeen

Climbing to his feet was awkward since he refused to let go of Caden, but he finally managed it and then faced Nero and Dare.

His Enforcers.

Shit, he really did have a pack.

"Call the cleaners and get them—"

Nero clapped him on the shoulder, a line of blood staining his ridiculously handsome face from the corner of his mouth to his Adam's apple. "We got this. Take care of him."

He gave them both an appreciative nod and then dragged Caden away from the living room and all of the blood and dead bodies. He steered them past the guest room that Caden had slept in the one night he'd been there and went all the way down to Quinten's.

He pushed the door open and then closed it quickly behind them.

"Caden, can you look at me?"

Caden shook his head, pressing in closer.

"Kitten, I just need to make sure that you're alright."

He could feel wetness on his neck, and it killed him that

he was crying, that all of this bullshit was bringing back some of the worst memories of his life. But he was grateful that his sweet mate hadn't had to actually be the one to kill Tiho.

In fact, Quinten was more than a little glad that he was the one who had gotten the pleasure. He would've been happy as long as the man was dead, but the fact that he was dead at *his* hands felt right in a primal way. He wasn't sure if it was a side effect of the spell still racing through him or if that's how he would feel once it wore off too.

He ran his fingers over the back of Caden's head and through his soft hair. He ignored the fact that he still had blood all over him and just did his best to try and soothe his mate.

Finally, Caden's breathing slowed, and he lifted his head to meet Quinten's gaze. "I'm okay."

"Are you sure?"

Caden nodded and looked down at himself. His nose wrinkled. "We both smell like Tiho though."

"Well, that's disgusting," Quinten said with a soft smile. "How do you feel about a shower?"

Caden nodded quickly and led the way into the bathroom.

Quinten kept his eyes on him as he stripped and got the water ready. As soon as Caden dropped his pants, his heart leapt into his throat.

"You're bleeding," he cried, shooting forward faster than he was used to and nearly taking them both out. Dropping to the tiled floor, he examined the hole from the bullet.

"Oh. Yeah, it's nothing."

"Nothing? He fucking shot you." He started to get up. "Dare!"

Caden snorted a laugh, but Quinten didn't see what was so damn funny. "Dare, we don't need you!" Caden

210

called out, and then it was his turn to clasp Quinten's face in his hands and hold him steady. "I'm fine. I'd be fully healed by the time we even got to the parking garage."

Quinten's brows furrowed. He knew that. Why was he panicking so much?

He looked down at the wound and started to get riled up all over again, even though he could tell that it was visibly smaller and had stopped bleeding.

He took a couple of deep breaths and climbed to his feet. "You're sure you're okay? Is the bullet still in there?"

"No," Caden said. "I felt it come out a little while ago."

"You shifters and your healing. It's amazing, but it's also gross."

Caden gasped, pretending to be offended, and shoved lightly at his chest, but Quinten grabbed a hold of his forearms and hauled him close. The water had heated up and was beginning to fill the bathroom with steam.

"We should get clean," Quinten said, but he didn't make a move, just stared into Caden's eyes.

"In a second."

Quinten nodded and waited.

"You called me your mate."

He smiled gently. "You were right about a lot of things, including me being a coward."

Caden shook his head quickly. "No, that was out of line."

"No, it wasn't," Quinten said firmly. He rested his hands low on Caden's hips. "I was scared. You scare me."

Caden sucked in a breath, but he didn't interrupt, watching Quinten with wide, hopeful eyes.

"The things I feel for you are scary to me. You make me vulnerable in a way I've refused to allow myself to be for a long time. But the idea of continuing to walk this earth without you by my side terrifies me even more. If you can forgive me—"

Caden was smiling and leaning in, pressing a kiss to his mouth before he could even finish.

He grinned against his mate's soft mouth. After getting a thorough taste, he pulled back. "Denying the facts because of my hang-ups won't change them," he said softly, slipping his hands down over the curve of Caden's ass.

"Facts plural?" Caden asked breathlessly.

"Yeah, kitten. Because not only are we fated for one another, but that ragtag group out there pretending like they aren't listening to us is my pack."

The way Caden cocked his head just a little and smiled wider let him know that at least Nero had laughed. Caden leaned into Quinten. "Should I call you Alpha Amato now?"

Quinten smiled, that magic inside him heating all over again. "No, just Alpha will do."

Caden nodded seriously, then grinned and jumped into the shower. Quinten followed behind, getting distracted as much as he did actual cleaning.

Eventually, he growled in frustration, his mate's hands *accidentally* brushing against his hard cock for the third time in as many minutes. The sound was deeper and sounded like a shifter's, but he didn't think too hard about that, too interested in chasing his mate out of the bathroom and into their bedroom. The spell would wear off eventually.

Caden barely got on the bed before Quinten was gripping his hips and flipping him over onto his back. Gently, he used his thumb to caress under one of Quinten's eyes. "This is an interesting look on you."

"Handy little spell from Ginger. She adapted it from something a witch in my brother's coven does for mates."

Caden's eyebrows shot up. "What does it do exactly?"

"It temporarily borrows magic from any nearby pack members to give me a boost in strength and speed."

"So basically a shot of shifter mojo straight into your veins."

Quinten grinned down at him. "Basically. It'll wear off though," he said, wanting to be clear about that in case Caden got ideas. "Probably not for a little while though."

"Then let's take advantage," Caden said, spreading his thighs to make more room for Quinten between them. "Bite me again. Use those cute little fangs on me, mate."

Quinten was turned on and affronted. "Little?"

Caden wiggled against him, and his annoyance evaporated. "Please, Alpha?"

Groaning, Quinten dropped his head and sucked in a deep breath right at the curve of Caden's neck. Fuck, he smelled like roses for some reason, and Quinten couldn't get enough, sucking huge lungfuls inside him, hoping to keep that scent with him long after the spell wore off.

Caden moaned, digging his fingers into Quinten's hair. "Lube first. Want you inside me when you bite me."

Shuddering, Quinten scrambled backward to grab the tube out of his bedside table. It was as close to fully bonding as they'd get. He just prayed it was enough for his mate.

"It is, Quin. You are more than enough."

He craned his head around to stare at Caden. His scent must have given him away, and he was grateful for the first time in his life. "Everything I have in me, I'll give to you, Caden. Every last piece."

Caden sat up and cupped his face, eyes shining. "I'll take it. It's all I've ever wanted. I'll never wish for more or grow bored. I'll never get frustrated at who or what you are. I'll love every single piece, and I'll protect them from anyone who'd try to hurt you, just like you protect me."

Cheeks damp, Quinten fell back onto his mate, shud-

213

dering as he held him and caressed him, letting Quinten quietly cry against his throat.

"I love all your pieces too, kitten," he whispered hoarsely.

Caden's hands tightened on him, his rose scent spiking all around him.

Lifting his head, he smiled. "That makes you pretty happy, huh?"

"So happy, mate."

Carefully, he kissed Caden, tasting him around his sharper-than-normal teeth and moaning when he arched against him, rubbing his still-hard dick against Quinten's stomach. Fuck, his mate really was perfect for him, always so needy and ready for him.

Their lips parted with a slick sound that made his gut clench. "You still want—"

"Goddess yes." Caden's fingers dug into his shoulders. "Can I... Can I bite you too?"

Scorching heat shot through him at the soft question. "Fuck, yes. Leave your mark on me, kitten."

Eyes glowing, Caden felt around him on the sheets until he found the lube and thrust it at Quinten's chest, moving him back in the process. He grabbed the back of his own thighs and pulled them up. "Hurry, Quin. Don't make me wait."

He didn't want to, but he had to get a taste of his mate with his temporarily enhanced senses. Darting forward, he ran his tongue straight up his cleft, all the way to the back of his tightly furled balls.

"Quin!"

"Fuck, you taste even better. Like roses and sex, kitten. You're going to turn me into a damn addict," he muttered, gripping Caden's plump cheeks and holding them wide apart so he could sink his tongue inside him.

He gave it a wiggle, knowing how much Caden loved that, and was rewarded with a heel slamming into his back.

"Ow," he grunted, lifting his head. "Not actually a superhuman down here. Be careful not to break your alpha, kitten."

"Shit, sorry. But for real, I will murder you in your sleep if you don't shove your fat dick inside me right fucking now."

Quinten raised his brows, holding Caden's eyes as he grabbed the lube once more and squirted some on his hand. "Well, we wouldn't want that."

Caden shook his head frantically, tipping his hips up to offer himself further.

Quinten didn't bother fingering him. His mate wanted it now, he'd get it. He doubted he'd hear a complaint, considering how much he loved when Quinten got rough with him.

Pressing inside his mate again shouldn't have been any different than it'd been yesterday—and yet, it was a million times better. He stared into his golden eyes, and he worked himself in all the way to the hilt, his emotions swirling inside him and turning into a tsunami that would need to escape.

Yesterday, he'd been terrified of what he felt when he was with Caden so intimately.

Today, he fucking cherished it.

"Good?"

"So good," Caden whispered, releasing his hold on his legs and wrapping them around Quinten. "Take me, mate."

He did. His hips moved faster than he normally could have, an added thrust of strength at the end of each slide inside, and his kitten moaned for more.

Sinking down, he threaded their fingers together and held Caden's hands to the bed, peppering kisses down his

215

neck. It was too good, everything dialed up to a hundred. He wasn't going to last.

But his mate had asked for one more thing.

When he reached the spot where Caden's neck met his shoulder, he gave the skin a long lick, and Caden shuddered.

"Yes, do it. Please."

He bared his teeth and struck. He'd expected the taste of copper to fill his mouth, but as Caden screamed and squeezed the come right out of his dick, he gulped greedily at the sweet rose flavor on his tongue.

There was a sharp pinch, and then pleasure shot through him all over again as Caden bit him. He didn't stop coming, his hips shuttling his dick forward again and again.

But then, something caught.

Brow furrowed, he tried to pull out, but Caden tightened his thighs, holding him in place. Quinten's eyes rolled to the back of his head as the base of his cock swelled and became sensitive, caught right at the entrance of Caden's hole.

His mate squeezed down on him.

"Fuck!" His head flew back, and pure white washed over his eyes.

When he could see again, Caden was lounging on the bed, looking satisfied and pleased with himself. "Interesting development."

Quinten was still panting heavily, and his *knot* was still locked inside his mate. "Ginger has some explaining to do."

The sweet sound of his kitten's happiness flowed around him, and he sighed, content in a way he'd never been his entire life.

Settling against Caden, he murmured, "Love you, mate."

"I love you, my alpha."

Epilogue

"He has no idea where he was being kept?" Rick asked—for the third time—sounding frustrated.

Quinten rolled his eyes. "Oh yes, that's right. He does, and I just forgot to mention it."

Kincaid growled, but it didn't impress him like it used to. "I'm just asking—"

"I know." He sobered, wanting to make sure the alpha knew he was taking things seriously. "If I find out anything new, I'll let you know. I promise."

Rick grunted. "This new, helpful version of you is hard to get used to."

"I've always been helpful. Just not to you." He leaned back in his desk chair, glancing out the window to see the sun was starting to set. His mate would be waiting for him. They'd come out to the house for the weekend and had plans for how they'd spend the evening. The freshly charged runes on his arm fucking tingled like they knew.

"That's been the problem, yeah."

Quinten rolled his eyes. "You didn't need it."

"You don't have to act like you've turned over a new leaf

for me, Amato. Just, you know, keep your hands out of the bloodiest stuff, and we can come to an arrangement."

Frustrated, Quinten pushed to his feet, ready to be done with the conversation. "This isn't a new leaf, Kincaid. This is who I've always been."

"You've always helped—"

"Yes, you condescending—" He stopped himself. "Look, people assuming I was the devil personified used to benefit me and the things I do, but the world is changing."

"I've heard," Rick muttered.

"So it's time for the Amato Pack to come out of the shadows and take our place with everyone else. Whatever you think of me, my people deserve that."

There was silence on the line for a while before Rick finally said, "Are you trafficking people?"

"What?" He scowled at his desk.

"Do you traffic people?"

"Of course not. What the hell, man?"

"There have been rumors..." Rick said mildly.

"Yeah, because I smuggle vampires in and run shifters out," he said, huffing. "I can't believe you were thinking about letting us join your do-gooders club when you thought I was a human trafficker."

"I wasn't sure—"

"Honestly, I'm shocked, and I'm not sure your Guardians are the right fit for us anymore," he added, grinning when Rick growled at him again.

"Alright, alright. You've proved your point. What about the one about how you force people to pay you for protection?"

"That one is true. It's a service we provide for small packs and covens."

"But you make them pay you," Rick said like he was proving some point.

"Yes, Rick. It's called running a business, not a charity. Seriously, man, how have you not bankrupted your pack?"

"Listen—"

"Actually, I have to go. My mate's waiting for me."

Rick huffed. "Mine too. I'll let you know if my people come up with any new information."

"I'll do the same."

He hung up and stared at his phone. What a difference a month could make. He'd been so sure that joining forces with the Kincaid Pack and Guardians would ruin what he'd built, but once Rick got over being an uptight asshole, he'd welcomed Quinten like any other alpha.

Sure, people still gave him some side-eye at being a human alpha, but then his alpha-mate or second-in-command would growl at them until they remembered their manners.

Dare loved doing that.

Speaking of...

"Dare!" He picked up the small dagger he kept on his desk as a letter opener.

The wolf stuck his head into the office, scarred brow raised.

"Excellent." He sliced open his thumb and pressed the blood to the runes.

"For fuck's sake," Dare grumbled, disappearing again.

"Better take the night off," he hollered as the spell coursed through him, strengthening his muscles and sharpening his senses. "Unless you want to overhear me knotting my—"

"Fucking stop!" Dare yelled back, slamming the front door behind him.

He chuckled. Who knew Dare could be such a prude. Just because he and his mate enjoyed using the side benefits of his wolfy second-in-command didn't mean he had to get all huffy. Ginger was the one who made the spell take the most traits from the closest shifter to him when he cast it.

He and Caden appreciated it though.

A lot.

His heightened ears picked up the sound of his mate laughing and darting into the hedge maze behind the house. Grinning around his sharp teeth, he stripped and grabbed the lube.

"Here I come, kitten."

Thank you for reading The Mobster's Mate!
This is the end of Quinten and Caden's journey... but not the end of the <u>whole</u> story.

If you're curious about what Quinten and Rick will do when they find the people who hurt Caden—and so many others— be sure to read my upcoming series: the Silver Oak Pack!

Wish you could have seen what Caden and Quinten got up to in the hedge maze? I've got a bonus epilogue with that steamy scene available for my newsletter subscribers!

A Note from Kiki

THANK YOU. THANK YOU. THANK YOU.

Thank you for reading *The Mobster's Mate*. If you enjoyed Quinten and Caden's story, please consider leaving a review to help other readers find their book!

Wanna never miss a release or sale?
Follow me on BookBub or on Amazon!

To always make sure you know what I'm working on, have the opportunity to read early copies of my books, and get freebies, subscribe to my newsletter!

Expand Your TBR!

Now that you've finished with The Mobster's Mate, you might like...

Sunshine (written with EM Lindsey) features an age gap, fated mates, a prince falling for his bodyguard, lots of possessiveness, and some interesting uses of a Siren's tail. The series has an over-arching plot and should be read in order.

Available in eBook, Paperback, & Kindle Unlimited.

Reckless is the first in my Leather & Chrome series which focuses on the Devil's Hands Motorcycle Club and the exploration of friendship and kink! Tank and CJ's story features a prison pen pal program, an age gap, exhibition-ism, and a tough biker only soft for his sweet virgin.

Available in eBook, Paperback, Audiobook, & Kindle Unlimited.

Also by Kiki Clark

Kincaid Pack Series

The Alpha and His King (Rick & Kai)

The Second and His Bonded (Kieran & Bennett)

The Deputy and His Enforcer (Robson & Marcus)

The Hunter and His Mates (Drake, Jamie, & Gabriel)

The Enforcer and His Heart (Nico & Keegan)

The Witch and His Doctor (Carter & Damien)

Kincaid Pack Coloring Book

Trident Agency Series (written with EM Lindsey)

Sunshine

Priest

Leather & Chrome Series

Reckless (Tank & CJ)

Temptation (Six & Ollie)

Yearning (Houston & Kenneth)

Joyful (Rooster & Emmett)

Possession (Tomas & Mason & Vinnie)

Blue Collar Hearts Series

Out In the Cold (Coop & Beau)

Laying Pipe (John & Lukas)

Banger (Kevin & Hank)

Forever Family Trilogy

Favor (Declan & Jeremy)

Easy (Simon & Jackson)

Faker (Samuel & Will)

Collected Works — *Best deal!*

Many of my books are also available in audio! Be sure to check out my website or Audible.com.

About the Author

A small-town Michigan girl, Kiki has enjoyed reading since she first picked up a YA fantasy as a child. After that, she devoured everything she could get her hands on and dreamed of one day writing her own books that touched people's hearts.

In 2020, she proudly joined the ranks of authors releasing character-driven, emotionally satisfying books showcasing that everyone deserves to find love.

To keep up-to-date with Kiki, sign up for her newsletter: http://www.kikiclark.com/newsletter.

Keep in touch by following her on any of these platforms:

facebook.com/kikiclarkauthor

instagram.com/kikiclark2017

amazon.com/author/kikiclark

bookbub.com/authors/kiki-clark

goodreads.com/kikiclark